amazon.co.uk

A gift from **Beth HELYER**

Enjoy your gift! From Beth HELYER

Gift note included with Polly's Story: 1890: Volume 1 (Swallowcliffe Hall)

Books by Jennie Walters:

The Swallowcliffe Hall *series:*

Downstairs:
Polly's Story, 1890
Grace's Story, 1914
Isobel's Story, 1939
Upstairs:
Eugenie's Story, 1893

For teens:
See You in my Dreams

www.jenniewalters.com

Swallowcliffe Hall

Isobel's Story

1939

Jennie Walters

Half Moon Press
London

Author's Note

Several people have helped in the writing of this book. I am particularly grateful to two of the original Kinder: Hermann Hirschberger, who so generously shared his experiences with me, and Lisa Vincent, who read my manuscript for accuracy and tone. Many thanks also to Wendy Whitworth and the Holocaust Centre, Beth Shalom (www.holocaustcentre.net); to Richard Drachman for granting permission to reproduce lines from his father Julian Drachman's poem, 'How Shall We Sing?' (from Just Now, for Instance: A Retrospective Selection of Ninety Poems, published by Stinehour Press, 1969); to Randall Bytwerk, who has made a study of Nazi propaganda, www.calvin.edu/academic/cas/gpa, for permission to reproduce his translation of Herman Esser's writing; to Sally Holloway for telling me so much about London in the 1930s; to Rachel Grange and Jolanta Henderson for advising on dialogue; to Harriet Stallibrass, as ever, for her helpful comments.

First published in Great Britain in 2007 by Simon and Schuster UK under the title *Shelter from the Storm*

Whilst we have tried to ensure the accuracy of this book, the author cannot be held responsible for any errors or omissions found therein. All rights reserved.

Copyright © Jennie Walters, 2007, 2011
Cover design by Amanda Lillywhite, www.crazypanda.com
Cover photographs copyright © Jennie Walters, 2011
ISBN-10: 1491294744
ISBN-13: 978-1491294741

Chapter One

We must hope for the best and prepare for the worst.
Prime Minister Neville Chamberlain on his return from meeting Adolf Hitler in Munich, September 1938

'BETTER TAKE EVERY JERSEY you've got,' Mum warned, dragging the battered leather suitcase off the top of her wardrobe. 'You don't know what cold is until you've spent a winter in that ice box of a place. And don't forget your gas mask, for Heaven's sake.'

I was going back with my granny to stay at Swallowcliffe Hall for a while so she could put some flesh on my bones and I could breathe fresh country air instead of London smog. 'Look at the poor girl! She's as pale as a ghost,' Gran had exclaimed when she'd arrived to stay with us for the holiday and found me dozing in Dad's old chair by the fire, wrapped up in a blanket. 'Well, that's tuberculosis for you.'

Swallowcliffe Hall

I'd only just got out of the sanatorium in time for Christmas. 'Aren't you the lucky one!' the nurses had said. I didn't feel so lucky, not after spending months in a hospital bed with no idea what was going on outside while my friends were all having fun without me. 'You haven't missed much,' Mum had said. 'The same old palaver about whether there'll be a war and the Prime Minister going off for a pow wow with Herr Hitler.'

I didn't like the idea of leaving Mum and my brothers, not with war on the horizon, but Swallowcliffe wasn't so very far away - only down in Kent - and I could probably get back on the train in an emergency, or they could come down and join us. Besides, there wasn't much choice. Mum had to go back to work in the new year and I still couldn't manage by myself. My legs felt wobbly if I stood up for too long, and the thump of Stan and Alfie's football in the back alley made my head pound like a roadmender's drill. Gran would look after me and when I felt better, she said, I could start helping her with odd jobs in the kitchen.

'Now then,' Mum had interrupted, 'you're not turning our Izzie into a kitchenmaid. She'll be back home and studying for School Certificate as soon as she's well.'

'I know,' Gran had replied, 'but she might as well keep herself busy in the meantime.'

You could see from Mum's face that she still

Isobel's Story

wasn't happy. She can't bear the thought of any of us going into service like she and her mother did when they were young. Gran had started working at Swallowcliffe Hall when she was my age and never left; she was cook/housekeeper now. We'd only visited the place once, Stan and me, around the time our father died (Alfie wasn't more than a few months old so he'd stayed behind with Mum). It must have been ten years ago, but I could remember a few things: climbing up a narrow wooden staircase that seemed to stretch on for ever, looking out of an attic window across miles of fields and woodland, standing in a jungly greenhouse and biting into a tiny, warm tomato which burst into sweetness on my tongue. When I forgot to worry, going off to Swallowcliffe with Gran seemed a wonderful idea. It'd be quiet there, and peaceful. I was sick of lying in bed, staring at the same four walls or trying to read while Stan and Alfie fought downstairs and the buses rumbled along our street. If only it wasn't for Hitler...

I watched Mum as she fiddled with the suitcase's rusty catches. 'Mum, if there *is* a war any time soon, you and the boys will come down as well, won't you? It'll be much too dangerous to stay in London.'

'We'll stick together one way or another, Izzie, I promise,' she said, sitting down beside me on the bed and smoothing a strand of hair behind my ear. 'Try not to fret so much. Mr Chamberlain's sorted things out for the moment.'

So why did we have to take our gas masks everywhere? Why were they still digging those mysterious trenches no one knew the reason for, and why were sandbags still piled up outside the town hall? Hitler wasn't really backing down and nobody knew for certain what he'd do next, no matter what the Prime Minister said. I wanted us all to be together in the country where it was safe.

I felt suddenly shy, sitting opposite Gran in the chilly railway carriage as we set off for the Hall, but at least we didn't have to talk. She had her knitting and I had my book - the latest in the *Chalet Girl* series. I'd grown out of the Chalet School books, really, but it was comforting to have something familiar from home in my haversack. Yet I couldn't settle to reading and gazed out of the window as the backstreets of London flashed by, trying to imagine what lay in store.

Gran caught my eye. 'Fancy a barley sugar?' She snapped open the clasp of her handbag and started rustling about inside it.

'If I bump into Lady Vye, should I curtsey?' I asked Gran when we were sucking away at our sweets. 'And what should I call her?'

'You can call her Lady Vye,' Gran said, 'or "ma'am", if you'd rather. And we don't go in for curtseying these days. If I took to bobbing about at my age, they'd have to get a winch to haul me up

Isobel's Story

again!' And she laughed.

I hope I look like Gran when I'm old. She has smooth, nut-brown skin even in the winter, crinkled and worn like an old leather glove; when she smiles, her face lights up and the years fall away. She patted my knee. 'Now don't worry so much. You won't be seeing a great deal of Lady Vye, anyway. The family aren't back from Scotland for a few days and then I expect she'll go straight up to London. She's not much of a one for the country. The children will be about, of course, although Master Tristan's due back at school soon so you may not even catch a glimpse of him.'

We knew something of the Vye children at home because Tristan, the oldest, was just a couple of years younger than Alfie, and my brothers always clamoured to hear the latest Master Tristan story whenever Gran came to visit. To us, he seemed like a cross between Little Lord Fauntleroy and Oliver Twist. He had two little sisters - twins of six, Miss Julia and Miss Nancy - but somehow they didn't hold the same fascination, being only girls and having more ordinary names.

'As soon as you're up to it, you can start with some easy jobs like cleaning the silver or mending linen,' Gran said, taking up her knitting again. 'And you might like to spend some time reading to the twins. The nursery maid keeps them clean and fed, but she's not got much imagination.' She sniffed.

'Sissy, her name is. You'll meet her soon enough.'

I leaned my head against the grimy window and gazed out, wondering about this strange, old-fashioned world of silver and linen and nursery maids - a world as foreign to me in its own way as the Austrian Tyrol, where the Chalet School was set. Now the railway line was running between row upon row of terraced houses with tiny concrete backyards like ours, the odd piece of washing half-frozen on a line. Here was a garden with a patch of lawn, big enough for an Anderson shelter covered over with turf like a miniature hill fort. Mum said we didn't need a bomb shelter outside anyway, not with our cellar, but what if the house was hit and we were trapped down there in the dark, with no one to hear us or know we were there? I picked up my book and tried to stop thinking. The next time I looked outside, the sooty landscape of cement and brick had given way to misty fields and oasthouses; we'd arrived in Kent.

We were met at Hardingbridge Station by the chauffeur and handyman at the Hall, Mr Oakes. He had a dour, craggy face with a smear of blood on the chin where he'd cut himself shaving, and was dressed in a flat cap and a tweed jacket with leather patches at the elbows. Apparently he'd only wear uniform when the family were at home. I didn't mind that at all, but I did feel horribly sick in the motor-car. It was only the second time I'd ever been taken out for

Isobel's Story

a drive. If we went anywhere at home, we took the bus or a tram, and I wasn't used to being shut up in a stuffy, jolting box. Luckily we'd only been going for ten minutes or so when Gran tapped on the glass partition between us and Mr Oakes in front, and he brought the car to a stop by the side of the road.

'I won't be long,' she said, opening the passenger door. I got out too, partly for a breath of air and partly because I didn't want to be left behind with silent Mr Oakes. We had arrived at a churchyard. I leaned against the car and watched Gran walk through the gate and down a path between the gravestones, clutching her bag with both hands. She has a bad knee and limps a little, so the glass cherries on her hat chinked together with every step. I don't like cemeteries - they give me the creeps - but the sight of my granny standing all alone by one of the graves, head bowed, made me follow her down the path. She took a little bunch of mistletoe and Christmas roses tied up with ribbon from her handbag and laid it against the headstone while I hovered around behind, not sure whether she wanted company.

'It's all right, dear,' Gran said, without turning round. 'You can come nearer if you like.'

'Iris Baker', read the inscription on the stone, '1869-1890'. That was ages ago! 'Was she a friend of yours?' I asked, realising it was a stupid question as soon as the words were out of my mouth. Iris Baker must have meant a lot to Gran if she was still visiting her grave nearly fifty years later.

She nodded. 'Iris took care of me when I first arrived at Swallowcliffe. She passed away around Christmas, so I usually pay my respects at this time of year.'

'Is Grandad buried here too?' I asked, looking at the neighbouring headstones.

'No, he's in the village churchyard at Stone Martin - much handier. I'll show you on Sunday.'

We stood for a while longer without speaking. I was thinking how little I really knew about Gran and the life she'd led when she was young. Or the life she led now, for that matter. Was she lonely, all on her own? Grandad had died about six years ago and, out of their four children, Mum was the only one near by. (Aunt Hannah was up in Yorkshire, Aunt Ivy had married an Australian soldier and had her own family out there now, while Uncle Tom had been killed in the war.) Mum had gone down to Swallowcliffe for Grandad's funeral - she'd left us with Mrs Jones next door for the day, saying it wasn't the time or place for noisy children - but why hadn't she visited more often since then?

I gave Gran's hand a squeeze. 'Don't be too sad.'

'I won't,' she said, 'but it's important to remember.'

She took my arm and we walked back to

Isobel's Story

the car together. Mr Oakes started up the engine without a word and we set off again with a sickening lurch. I felt tired and low for the rest of the journey, as though the damp fog had seeped out of the graveyard and into my heart. Perhaps that was why the Hall made such an impression on me at first, looming out of the mist like Sleeping Beauty's castle. Several windows were boarded up, and the house stared blankly down as though determined not to show any interest in our arrival. The gravel drive sweeping up to the main entrance was studded with thistles, while bright green moss carpeted a flight of stone steps leading to an overgrown lawn. There didn't seem to be anyone about, apart from a large black bird waddling stiff-legged over the sodden grass which took off with an irritable 'caw' when Mr Oakes slammed the car door shut. He lifted our suitcases down from the luggage rack and led the way through a blue-painted door at the side of the house.

'We'll go straight upstairs so you can rest after the journey,' Gran told me as we followed him down the corridor inside. 'At least you'll have a few days to settle in before the family come back from Scotland. Your room's next door to mine, so you won't feel lonely, and when you've had a lie-down I'll show you where everything is and tell you what's what.'

By now we were climbing up a flight of stairs at the end of the hall. There was no carpet and they were quite steep. 'Can you manage, Gran?' I asked.

'Of course I can, dear. One flight of stairs isn't too much trouble. Mind you, I'd have a struggle getting up to the attic where we used to sleep when I was a girl - you'll have to explore that on your own. I've got a lovely room now opposite the nursery, and there's a bathroom we share with Sissy and the children. It's all very comfortable, you'll see.'

We had come to a bend in the staircase. A flight of three or four stairs on the right opened out into another, longer corridor with doors on each side. Mr Oakes strode off down it, deposited Gran's case outside the first door on the right, and mine outside the next one along. 'Thank you, Mr Oakes,' she said. 'And thank you again for meeting us.'

'You're welcome, Mrs S.' They were the first words I'd heard him speak. 'Miss.' He tipped his cap and marched back down the corridor.

'Here we are.' Gran opened the door to my bedroom and I followed her inside with my suitcase. The room was large, with pale green walls and a swirly red carpet. There were a few pieces of furniture cast adrift in it: a chair covered in faded flowery cotton, a white enamelled bedsteads made up with sheets, blankets and an eiderdown, and an oak chest of drawers in the window alcove. It was also cold. Incredibly cold. You could see your breath in a cloud on the air.

'Oh, that dozy Eunice! I wrote to tell her when

Isobel's Story

we were coming back. She was meant to have had a fire going in here all day!' Gran picked up the coal tongs and started struggling down on one knee by the fireplace.

'Don't worry,' I said, taking the tongs out of her hand and guiding her towards the door. 'I think I will have that rest now, if you don't mind.'

A wave of exhaustion and homesickness had suddenly washed over me. Not bothering with the fire, when Gran had gone I kicked off my shoes and climbed into bed under the blankets and quilt in my thick tweed coat, beret and gloves. So many empty rooms in that huge house, and only one of them filled by me! I felt like the beating heart in a sleeping, frozen body. Then I fell asleep myself, and dreamed about all sorts of extraordinary things. I dreamed Mum was running after me with my gas mask, but when I opened the cardboard box it was full of wriggling worms. I dreamed Mr Oakes came to fetch me from the station in a bus, but I didn't have any money for the fare. I dreamed I was following two girls down a country lane in summer. I called after them, and one of the girls looked back. It was Gran. 'Have you met my friend, Iris?' she said, but when the second girl turned around, she had no face, only two deep black holes for eyes.

This was so terrifying that I woke up with a start, bathed in a cold sweat - and knew immediately that I was not alone in the room. It was almost completely dark by now, but somebody was watching me, I felt certain. Watching and waiting. Yes! There, by the door, the blackness had puddled into a square, solid shape. The breath caught in my throat and my heart thumped so heavily it hurt my chest. Then the shape spoke. 'Who are you?' it said. And another voice chimed in, 'What are you doing in our house?'

So that was how I first met Miss Nancy and Miss Julia. The family had come home unexpectedly and, down in the kitchen, my granny was having kittens because none of the beds was aired.

Chapter Two

Make-up? Of course you must. Pale lifeless cheeks don't give you glamour. Use Snowflake Blush Cream, and be radiant with the natural colour that men adore. In four very alluring shades – Blonde, Brunette, Medium and Tangerine.
Advertisement in *Miss Modern* magazine, January 1939

ALL I DID FOR THOSE FIRST few weeks at the Hall was lie in bed all morning and then spend the afternoon sitting outside in a deckchair, wrapped in a moth-eaten fur coat from the dressing-up chest with a rug over my knees. As long as it wasn't raining, Gran insisted on me getting plenty of fresh air and I didn't complain because it usually seemed colder inside the house than out. The only warm room was the kitchen, with its huge black range that Mr Oakes stoked up with coke every day. As soon I started feeling stronger, I'd sit down there in the mornings and Gran would find me a few little jobs to do: peeling vegetables, kneading bread, polishing the odd piece of silver that Mr Huggins, the butler, hadn't got around to. Sometimes I'd take Wellington, the Vyes' chocolate Labrador, for a walk. My appetite had come back with a vengeance, and everything at Swallowcliffe was so delicious. Each morning we had crispy bacon or ham with Gran's homemade bread, and later on Mr Oakes would bring through a trugload of vegetables from the kitchen garden. The butcher's sausages tasted completely different from the flabby pink ones we ate at home ('dead men's fingers', Stan and Alfie call them), and butter from the farm dairy was so creamy and sweet you could polish off half a pound all by itself.

By the middle of my second month, it felt as though I'd been living at Swallowcliffe for years. One Saturday afternoon, Gran sent me on an errand to the village shop and I decided to take Nancy and Julia with me for a treat since Sissy had the day off. Something about the shopkeeper, Mr Tarver, made me feel uncomfortable, so perhaps I wanted some moral support as well. He had cold eyes and a false smile, and he knew everyone's business because he was an ARP warden. 'Air Raid Precautions', that's what ARP stands for. I'd once seen Mr Tarver kitted

Isobel's Story

out in an ARP armband and metal helmet, berating an old lady who hadn't come to him yet for her gas mask. He'd even ridden up to the Hall and told Gran she should start criss-crossing the windows with brown tape in case they were blown in.

'We must be prepared for all eventualities, Mrs Stanbury.' He'd bared his teeth in a fearsome grin. 'I trust you've begun measuring up for blackout material.'

To be honest, I wouldn't have wanted to go anywhere near the village shop if it hadn't been for the boy who helped behind the counter. The first time I saw him, I dropped my change all over the floor. There was something so startlingly vivid about his black curly hair, pale skin and sharp cheekbones that you couldn't help staring. Gran happened to let slip that he was German when he delivered our weekly order one day, and that was mysterious in itself. What was a German boy doing over here when his country was at loggerheads with ours? And how had he ended up in Mr Tarver's dark Aladdin's cave of groceries? I wasn't very good at talking to boys, but looking at him made a trip to the shop a lot more exciting.

And then Julia spoilt everything. 'We don't like that boy,' she announced in a loud whisper, pointing at him so there could be no confusion. 'He's a German spy.'

Just like that, right in the middle of the shop!

I could have killed her, except that would have drawn even more attention to us and I was hoping by some miracle that no one had heard what she'd said. Mr Tarver was busy with another customer - Miss Murdoch, the vicar's sister - and you can bet she did; she has bat's ears. I knew that because, the week before, she'd turned around from playing the organ and glared at two girls who were whispering at the back of the church. So I settled for frowning ferociously at Julia to stop her saying anything else.

The boy was reaching down a packet of fancy tea with a long pole that had a hook on the end. Mr Tarver's shelves were a work of art, with every tin, jar and packet arranged in intricate patterns, and the whole shop smelt rich and spicy as a fruitcake. It was even more crammed with goods than usual because the back storeroom had been cleared out and turned into a wardens' post. There were maps on the walls, an electric fire and a kettle for Mr Tarver and Mr Williams from the garage to make tea when they were on official warden duty.

The boy turned around with the tea in his hand, put it down on the counter and gave us a look. My face grew hot.

'Will that be all, Miss Murdoch?' Mr Tarver asked, a faint sheen of sweat glistening on his double chins. 'Shall I have your order sent round to the vicarage, or will you take the items now?'

The 'order' consisted of a paper bag of custard

creams, weighed out from a large tin, and the tea. 'I'll take them with me,' she said, stowing the shopping in her basket and getting up from the chair by the counter. 'I only popped in because I happened to be passing. The body requires sustenance as well as the soul, Mr Tarver, and my poor brother is at home wrestling with a sermon.'

'Oh, very good.' He laughed as though she'd made the funniest joke in the world and reached for a large black book on the counter top. 'I'll add them to your account.'

'When can we choose our sweets?' Nancy asked in a piercing voice, tugging at my hand.

Both Miss Murdoch and Mr Tarver looked round. 'Patience is a virtue, Miss Nancy,' Miss Murdoch said - which was clever of her, since Nancy and Julia are identical twins. Sometimes I find it hard to tell them apart, even now. They have the same grey eyes, the same dusting of freckles and the same explosion of curly fair hair that takes Sissy ages to brush in the morning. Nancy has a chicken pox scar over her right eyebrow, and that's the only difference between them, so far as I can make out.

'See you on Tuesday, Isobel,' Miss Murdoch said as she went by. Gran had volunteered me for a first aid evening class in the village hall, run by the Women's Voluntary Service, and Miss Murdoch took the register. I enjoyed the bandaging but now we were learning about the effects of different gases and that was horrible. I was considering pretending to be ill next week and coughed hollowly, hoping Miss Murdoch would remember that later.

At last it was our turn to be served. 'May I have two pounds of prunes, please?' I could see the boy in the corner of my eye, wiping down the bacon slicer, and hoped he wasn't listening. There was something embarrassing about prunes.

Mr Tarver waited until the door had closed behind Miss Murdoch with a jangling of its bell. 'Cash or account?' he asked abruptly.

'Account,' I answered, stammering slightly. Gran hadn't given me any money; Mr Tarver came up to the Hall at the end of each month for the bill to be settled and we were well into February now. Why did he need to ask?

He made a great performance of flicking over the pages in the black book until he came to the right one. Then he ran one podgy finger down the line of figures, frowning, and shook his head. 'Sorry, young lady. There's money owing since before Christmas and I can't give you any more credit. It'll be cash only until this account's paid off, I'm afraid.'

Now I was blushing to the roots of my hair. Mr Tarver straightened up and stared at us unpleasantly, the striped apron straining over his chest. Behind him, the German boy stared too.

'So, do you want those prunes or not?'

'How much are they?' I asked, feeling for the

purse in my pocket and wishing I could fall through the floor. I had sixpence of my own money to buy Nancy and Julia some ha'penny chews and a blank exercise book for myself. (I'd decided to start writing a diary.)

'Fourpence a pound.'

'I'll have a pound and a half then, please,' I said with as much dignity as I could muster. Gran needed the wretched things; Lady Vye was throwing a dinner party that night and she'd suddenly decided to serve devils on horseback as a savoury (which was prunes wrapped in bacon, apparently). I couldn't go back to the Hall without them.

Nancy pulled my arm again, sensing that something was wrong. 'What about our sweets?'

'Hush. We'll buy some sweets another day,' I told her, in a tone of voice that meant it'd be more than her life was worth to kick up a fuss. She narrowed her eyes and stuck out her lower lip but, thank goodness, nothing more.

The prunes lay glistening like plump black beetles in a glass jar on the shelf. Mr Tarver took the jar down, put a square of blue paper on the scales and tipped out a clump of them, adding one and then another with a pair of tongs until he reached exactly the right weight. Then he folded the paper into a neat parcel and pushed it across the counter to me. 'Will that be all?'

'For today, thank you.' I gave him the money,

took the prunes and dragged Nancy and Julia out of the shop. I was never going back there again.

'Why couldn't we have our sweets? Why was that man so horrid?' Julia demanded, dragging her feet along the pavement. 'We've walked all this way …'

'… for nothing!' Nancy finished the sentence for her, which was a habit of theirs.

'You always have a walk in the afternoon,' I said, 'and it's not even raining, so cheer up. And don't scuff your shoes or Nanny will be cross.' (Sissy's known to them as Nanny, even though she is no more than a 'slip of a thing', as my granny puts it.)

You might have thought my humiliation was complete, but worse was to come. I heard a call and turned around to see the German boy hurrying after us. 'I don't like - ' Julia began.

'Shh! We know that already,' I hissed.

'Excuse me,' the boy began, slightly out of breath. 'Excuse me, but the little girl must give back the sweets.'

It was an intriguing accent: soft, but very precise. I'd never heard a German person speaking English before. We'd seen newsreels of Hitler at the cinema, but of course he'd always been ranting away in his own language. (It would have given them all a shock if he'd suddenly started speaking English, wouldn't it?)

Isobel's Story

Still, this was adding insult to injury. 'She hasn't got any sweets,' I replied stiffly. 'We spent all our money on prunes.'

'No, she took them,' he said, pointing at Nancy. 'Now she must give them back.'

Nancy had turned bright red, but she didn't say anything. 'Nancy, tell him you aren't a thief,' I ordered. Not a word in response. And then I noticed that both her hands in their blue woollen gloves were clenched into fists. 'Nancy?' My stomach sinking, I gave her shoulder a little shake.

We were all staring at her. Slowly, slowly, she uncurled her fingers - and there in the palm of each hand lay three fruit chews, their pink and orange wrappers glowing against the bright blue wool. Most of the sweets were out of her range in glass jars, but there'd been an open box of chews on the counter; she must have raided it while Mr Tarver had his back to us, fetching the prunes.

I could hardly believe my eyes. 'Oh, you naughty girl!'

'I was going to share them with Julia,' she said. 'They weren't all for me.'

'That's not the point.' I took a deep breath, wondering where to begin.

'You must tell her it's wrong to take things,' the boy said.

'Don't worry, I will.' But that was only the start of it; Nancy would have to be marched back to the shop, made to hand over the sweets and say sorry to Mr Tarver. I could hardly bear to think how awful that would be.

The boy held out his hand. 'I will take them back, if you like. Mr Tarver did not see. But you will tell her, won't you?'

I hesitated, but only for a split second. 'Of course. Thank you very much - that's decent of you.' He'd saved our bacon twice: once for not ratting on Nancy in front of Mr Tarver, and now this. But what must he have thought of me?

'It's all right. Enjoy your prunes.' He smiled and suddenly the sun sailed out from behind a cloud, turning everything clear and golden.

'You must know it's wrong to steal,' I said to Nancy as we trailed up the long drive to the Hall. 'What do you think people will say? "There goes naughty little Nancy Vye, who takes things that don't belong to her"?'

She was stomping along with a pixie hood buttoned under her chin and a gas mask slung in its cardboard box around her neck - quite unrepentant. 'No, they won't. They'll say, "There goes poor little Nancy Vye, who never has any treats or nice things."'

'Listen,' I said, squatting down to her level, 'you're a very lucky girl. You have plenty to eat, and warm clothes, and lots of toys to play with. There are children in London who don't have shoes to

Isobel's Story

wear, not even in winter.' At the school where Mum taught, they collected spare pennies through the year to buy boots for the children who'd go barefoot otherwise. Nancy ought to realise how hard times were for some people. 'Anyway, there's no excuse for stealing. It's wicked, and if you carry on like this you'll get into very bad trouble and maybe even end up in prison. I shall have to tell Stanny, you know.' ('Stanny' is what they call my grandmother - Mrs Stanbury being quite a mouthful for a six-year-old.) There was no point threatening to tell Sissy.

That hit home. 'Oh, please don't, Isobel! Don't tell Stanny. I'll never, ever take anything again, I promise - cross my heart and hope to die.'

They love Gran; being allowed to come into the kitchen and help her make a cake or biscuits is a huge treat. In fact I didn't really want to tell my granny what Nancy had done because she worried enough about the twins as it was. 'They're turning into little savages and Her Ladyship won't take a blind bit of notice. A proper governess is what they need, not some village girl they can run rings around. See if you can keep them on the straight and narrow while you're here, Izzie.'

I think I'd managed to convince Nancy that a life of crime wasn't worth the candle by the time we'd walked back from the village. We hung up our outdoor things in the downstairs cloakroom and I took the girls upstairs where Sissy was waiting with their nursery tea. Leaving the twins to their milk and bread and butter, I went back down to give Gran my shopping and tell her what Mr Tarver had put me through to get it.

'The cheek of the man!' She stared down at the parcel of prunes, lying innocently between us on the scrubbed wooden table. 'How could he say such a thing? He was up here last week for Her Ladyship to settle the bill.'

'Maybe she only gave him some of the money,' I suggested.

'Was there anyone else in the shop at the time?' Gran asked.

I shook my head. 'Miss Murdoch had gone by then.'

'We should be grateful for small mercies, I suppose. Don't tell Eunice, whatever you do, or it'll be round the village quicker than greased lightning.' Eunice was the house-parlourmaid, who went home at the end of each day rather than living in - much to Gran's suspicion. She sank into a chair and pushed the blue-paper package away from her across the table. 'Dear lord! That it should come to this.'

I wanted to tell Gran that Mr Tarver was a horrible old man and she shouldn't take any notice of him, but she has firm views about young people respecting their elders and betters so I kept quiet, filled the kettle and put it on the hot plate to boil. Mrs Jeakes, the kitchen cat, glared at me from her

Isobel's Story

warm basket next to the range. I picked her up, feeling her body stiffen in outrage at the liberty, but she consented to be tickled under the chin for a few seconds before struggling out of my arms.

'The suppers and dances we used to have at Swallowcliffe before the war!' Gran said, a faraway look in her eyes. 'If only you could have seen the place then, Izzie, full of life and elegant conversation. All the ladies so beautifully dressed, and the gentlemen so handsome and charming: the very cream of society. Roaring fires in every room, and the dishes that came out of the kitchen would make your mouth water just to look at them. There'd be tradesmen queuing for hours to see the cook - it was a privilege to supply the Hall in those days. And to think that now we can't even run an account at the village shop! Well, I shall have to speak to Her Ladyship about it tomorrow. No sense raising the matter tonight.'

'Don't worry, Gran, I'm sure it's just a misunderstanding. Have you got time for a cup of tea?'

She looked at the clock. 'I should have, if you'll be a love and peel some potatoes for me. Mind you wash your hands, though. Goodness knows where that cat's been.'

'So, what's for dinner this evening?' I asked Gran when we'd had our tea and I was wrist-deep in potato peelings at the scullery sink.

'Leek and potato soup to start, then scalloped oysters, beef with a red-wine sauce and queen's pudding to follow. Not forgetting the savoury, of course. I could live without messing about with devils on horseback, I must say, but Her Ladyship's determined everything has to be perfect.'

'Because she wants to impress a certain person, that's why.' Eunice, the house-parlourmaid, had suddenly materialised behind us. She often turned up unexpectedly like that. Suddenly you'd turn around and there she was, but looking so bland and inscrutable that you couldn't possibly accuse her of eavesdropping. She reminded me of one of those wooden Russian dolls that nest inside each other: black hair parted in the middle, dark button eyes set in a round face and a comfortable, plumpish body - full of secrets.

Gran refused to be drawn; she was made of sterner stuff than me. 'Now then, Eunice, haven't you got enough to think about without filling that empty head of yours with gossip?'

'Who's coming tonight?' I asked, hoping for a clue, but Eunice was sulking so Gran answered my question.

'Nobody much. A Dowager Duchess - she's the only title - along with some artist friend of His Lordship's, and a few other couples to make up the numbers. One gentleman "in business" apparently, whatever that means. Trade, I shouldn't wonder. Oh, and Major Winstanley, so Mr Huggins had better make sure the whisky decanter's full. Have you seen Mr Huggins, Eunice?'

'He's in the dining room, finishing off the table,' she said huffily. 'Well, I've done the fires and tidied the drawing room so I'm going to have a sit-down for five minutes. We shall be up late and my chilblains are giving me gyp already.'

'Run and find Mr Huggins for me, would you, Izzie?' Gran asked. She put a china jug in my hands. 'Remind him the Major's coming, and could you ask for some red wine for cooking? Nothing too fancy. Don't worry, nobody's about - the Vyes'll be changing for dinner.'

I walked along the corridor past the butler's pantry and servery, then scuttled out into the hall. Going outside the servants' quarters usually made me nervous (it was the thought of bumping into Lady Vye unexpectedly around a corner) but the house was looking so beautiful in the gathering dusk that I couldn't help loitering for a while to look around. The huge marble staircase seemed to float up through the gloom like some ghostly stairway to heaven and, far above my head, the round skylight window framed a circle of inky velvet. Daylight is too harsh for Swallowcliffe: all you can see is faded upholstery, dark shapes on the wallpaper where paintings used to hang, scuffed and peeling paintwork. When evening falls, lamps cast flickering shadows over cracks in the walls and the place becomes suddenly magical and mysterious.

Then a door slammed upstairs, and I remembered my errand. In the dining room, Mr Huggins was darting around the mahogany table like a humming bird, straightening cutlery and flicking away any specks of dust with a linen cloth. There were three crystal glasses at every place and enough gleaming knives, forks and spoons to last a week of meals. (Thank goodness it wouldn't be me having to work out which ones to use!) A name card in a silver holder had been put beside each starched white linen napkin and two huge silver candelabra stood in the middle of the table, along with pots of white orchids from the greenhouse. I could smell their sweetness in the air, mixed up with beeswax polish and woodsmoke from the fire.

'Quite something, isn't it?' Mr Huggins had noticed me during one of his swoops on the table. Usually he's the very picture of dignity, slow and solemn, but that evening he was practically skipping about. 'Reminds me of the old days. Dinner parties were nothing out of the ordinary then, oh no. Run of the mill, you might say. And how is everything in the kitchen? I trust Mrs S is performing her usual miracle.'

'Yes, Mr Huggins. The menu sounds lovely. She's sent me to beg some red wine for cooking, if you can spare any. And she says did you know that

Isobel's Story

Major Winstanley's one of the guests?'

'Indeed I did, young lady. The decanters are brimming and I've fetched an extra bottle of single malt from the cellar in case of emergencies. We are prepared for everything! Now come along to the pantry with me and we'll fill that jug.'

I followed Mr Huggins back to the butler's pantry which he unlocked with a key from the pocket of his green baize apron, humming under his breath. Every surface seemed to be covered in bottles, and several cut-glass decanters stood about with silver name labels on chains around their necks. 'Whisky' was certainly full to overflowing, dribbling into a puddle on the tray. The cellar book lay open on a table, its pages splattered with a trail of purple droplets, while cloths soaked up another spillage on the floor.

'Brigade headquarters,' said Mr Huggins, sniffing up the winey air with great satisfaction. 'The command centre of the operation!' He reached for an unlabelled bottle beside the sink which had already been uncorked. 'This should do the job.' The wine splashed in a gurgling crimson stream into my jug. 'And a couple of inches left over - criminal to waste them.' In a second, he'd fetched two small tumblers from the cupboard and filled them too. I noticed his hand was shaking slightly. 'Join me in a toast, my dear. We shall drink to the success of the evening!'

I'd never tasted wine before, but Mr Huggins seemed in such a jolly mood that it would have been a shame to disappoint him. 'To the success of the evening,' we chorused, and clinked glasses. Ugh! I'd sooner have drunk cough medicine.

Back in the kitchen, Gran was opening oysters with a silver knife. 'Was everything all right out there?' she asked as I handed over the jug.

'I'll say. You should see Mr Huggins!' I told her. 'He's positively dancing on air.'

'Hmm,' she said, and looked worried.

Chapter Three

It isn't clever to suffer cold feet in miserable silence. Natty ankle socks and stout brogues are very comfortable, they can be very smart and always look so intellectual.
From *Miss Modern* magazine, April 1939

'I THINK THAT'S EVERYTHING.' Gran stood, hands on hips, surveying the table. The soup was made, the oysters sat in their scallop shells, waiting till the last minute to join the beef that was sizzling in the top oven, the potatoes were coming to a boil, and the carrots and cabbage were in saucepans ready to be cooked. 'How are you getting on with the prunes, lovie?'

'Nearly done. It was a good idea to cut them in half.' I was wrapping the prunes in rashers of bacon and threading them on a skewer; a fiddly

Swallowcliffe Hall

job, but good to sit in the toasty warm kitchen with something easy to do.

Gran looked at the baking tray and sniffed. 'Hardly worth the effort. I might whip up a few cheese straws to bulk them out if there's time.' She reached for the flour tin. 'The company should be arriving before long. Oh, where's that Eunice?'

'Here, Mrs S,' she said, gliding into the room and making us both jump.

'Good,' Gran said. 'Will you keep an eye on Mr Huggins for me? Something tells me he's brewing up.'

'What do you mean, Gran?' I asked, when Eunice had gone. 'Brewing up for what?'

'Grate some cheese for me, dear, if you've finished the prunes,' she said by way of a reply. 'And don't ask so many questions.'

'But why does Mr Huggins need an eye kept on him?' I persisted, coming back from the larder. 'He seemed on top form to me.'

She sighed. 'Oh, all right, then. You'll probably find out soon enough anyway. Mr Huggins had a hard time of it in the war. His nerves aren't what they were and sometimes he gets a little ... over-excited, you might say. When that happens, he'll come down to earth with an almighty bump and it's the last thing we need tonight.'

In less than five minutes Eunice was back; I'd never seen her move so fast. 'I can't find him

Isobel's Story

anywhere,' she panted. 'He's not in the hall, the dining room, the drawing room or the pantry, and not in his room, neither. I think he must be ... you know.' She pointed downwards with a meaningful look.

'Oh, good heavens above!' Gran wiped her hands on a drying-up cloth and looked at the clock. 'Well, we can't leave him there. You'll have to go and fetch him. Take Isobel - you won't be able to manage on your own.'

Eunice seized my arm and pulled me out of the kitchen by the side door. She hurried me along the passage and then opened a door under the stairs that I'd never noticed before. A flight of steps stretched before us into the pitch black. 'Mind you don't fall,' she warned. 'It's steep, and there's no stair rail.'

How could I begin to tell her? This was my worst nightmare: being shut in a confined space in the darkness. I've the sanatorium to thank for that - or more particularly, the iron lung which stood in its own special room in the hospital. It was meant to help you breathe, though nobody ever explained exactly how. You lay in the thing and a close-fitting lid was brought down over your body with a mask and breathing tube attached to your face. I never had to be put inside it, thank goodness, but the girl in the bed next to me did and I can still hear her screaming as they dragged her off. It gave us all the heebie-jeebies.

'Eunice, I'm sorry but I can't go down there,' I said, hating myself for being so feeble. 'I'm afraid.'

She turned around and shot me an unsympathetic look. 'Well, you'd better buck up and get un-afraid pretty sharpish. This is an emergency. Anyway, there's a light burning at the bottom. Hold on to my apron strings and you'll be all right.'

So that was that. She grabbed my hand, tucked it through the sash of her apron where it was tied at the back, and set off down the stairs with me in tow. There was no time to kick up a fuss; all I could do was cling on for dear life, fix my eyes on her broad back in front of me and try not to think about anything else. The air smelt fusty and stale, and somewhere near the bottom of the steps a strand of something damp floated across my face. I couldn't help gasping and tasted it sooty in my mouth.

'Nearly there,' Eunice said over her shoulder. 'Keep going. Look, there's the light.'

We stepped out on to the level and I saw a couple of dim bulbs hanging from the cellar's low, vaulted ceiling. The walls and floor were hewed from rough stone, and all along one side were stone cubbyholes: most of them bare but some containing a few cobwebby bottles that looked hundreds of years old. Three or four iron-banded wooden barrels lay against the other wall, one upended and empty.

'You might as well get used to it down here,' Eunice whispered (something about the place made

Isobel's Story

you want to lower your voice). 'This is where we'll be if the German bombers come over - the Vyes and us lot all hugger mugger together. I wonder what they'll make of that?'

I couldn't speak. In the silence, we both became aware of a low keening sound that made the hairs on the back of my neck stand up. Eunice stiffened, peering into the gloom. 'There he is.' She took my hand again; her own was clammy and I suddenly realised she was frightened too. It made me feel better, in an odd sort of way. 'Come on, we'll have to go and get him.'

I don't know how we made it from one end of the cellar to the other, but we must have done somehow because suddenly there we were, looking down at a huddled shape on the floor that was Mr Huggins - although a very different Mr Huggins from the one I'd seen upstairs an hour before. It was as though someone had opened a valve and let all the air out of him. He was sitting against the wall, rocking his head against his knees and moaning quietly. 'Can't do it,' I heard him say. 'No use, no use at all. No use to anyone.'

'Don't worry, Mr Huggins.' Eunice bent over him. 'You come along with us.'

She took one arm and I took the other, and together we hoisted him to his feet. He wasn't a big man but a dead weight all the same, and it was hard work, half-dragging, half-carrying him back to the stairs. We stopped at the foot of them to catch our breath.

'Phew!' Eunice said, wiping her face with the back of her hand. 'Now we'll have to go single file.'

She hooked her arms under Mr Huggins' shoulders and started heaving him up backwards, feeling gingerly behind with her foot for each next step. I carried his legs and tried to take as much of his weight as possible, to help her. We had to go slowly; Eunice stumbled once and nearly fell, which gave us an awful fright. Each time she hoisted Mr Huggins up, I could tell by the strain on her face and the noise she made that the effort was nearly killing her. He was silent now. All you could hear in the darkness was the two of us grunting and groaning, and the thump of his body against stone.

At last - at long, long last - we reached the top and staggered out into the light of the corridor. Between us we propped Mr Huggins against the wall, and Eunice straightened her lopsided cap with one hand. 'Well, I'm not going back down there in a hurry. Let's get him to his room for a lie-down. He won't be doing any more work tonight.'

So what would become of Her Ladyship's dinner party now?

'Mr Oakes?' Eunice stared at Gran. 'You'll never get him to pass for an indoor servant, not in a month of Sundays.'

Isobel's Story

'We don't have a choice,' Gran replied sharply. 'Somebody has to carve the beef and I should think he's capable of taking everyone's coats and telling them dinner is served.'

'What's he going to wear?' Eunice asked. 'He'll never fit into Mr Huggins's livery.'

'I've found a tailcoat in the linen room that'll probably do - he's putting it on now in the pantry. There's a clean apron here for you, too. I knew you'd get yours in a mess, down in that filthy cellar. And uniform for Isobel.'

'Me?' I asked, startled, as Gran handed me a neatly folded parcel of black silk with a white cap and apron on top. 'But I'm going to be staying in the kitchen with you, aren't I?'

'Not tonight, dear. Eunice can't manage on her own if she's to wind up Mr Oakes and point him in the right direction. You don't mind, do you?'

'No, I suppose not,' I stammered. 'But I probably won't make a very good parlourmaid.'

'Just do as Eunice says and you'll be fine.' Gran sent me off to wash and change with a gentle push. 'And don't tell your mother, whatever happens, or she'll have forty fits. Quickly now! There isn't a minute to spare.'

'It's all very well,' Eunice grumbled as we hurried along to the drawing room a little while later. 'Nobody asks *me* whether I mind all this toing and froing and rooting about in cellars. I shouldn't have to put up with it and I won't for much longer, that's the honest truth. Everything's topsy turvy - '

This monologue was interrupted by a ring on the doorbell. 'Oh no! Somebody's here already.' She shrank back against the wall. 'Where's Mr Oakes?'

We were overtaken by a tall figure loping past us down the hall. Mr Oakes was wearing evening tails but the trousers that went with them weren't nearly long enough and flapped around his ankles, revealing a pair of scuffed black shoes. His hair had been brushed down flat with water and stood out around his head like nothing so much as a stiff black lampshade. 'Look at him,' Eunice whispered. 'Frankenstein's long-lost brother.'

Mr Oakes opened the front door, letting in a blast of cold air. 'Yes?' He seemed reluctant to let anyone through it.

'Oh, good heavens,' Eunice said. 'Stay here, Izzie, while I rescue the company, and then follow me into the drawing room.'

Now my legs turned to water. Lord and Lady Vye would be sitting there, waiting for their guests to arrive. What would they say when they saw me dressed up as a parlourmaid, let alone Mr Oakes in his Frankenstein outfit? But Eunice was already discreetly tugging him back from the door by his tails, forcing him to open it wider - and our first couple for dinner stepped over the threshold.

'Huggins not about?' enquired the red-faced

gentleman, shrugging off his overcoat and dumping it in Mr Oakes' unresponsive arms while Eunice helped his wife out of her furs.

'On holiday, Major Winstanley,' she replied promptly, adding the stole to Mr Oakes' load. 'Would you care to come this way?' And she started off towards the drawing room.

Straightening my cuffs, I took a deep breath and followed on behind the Winstanleys, trying to look as much like a proper parlourmaid as possible. The black frock smelt of mothballs and didn't fit me very well, but Gran had hidden that by bunching up the silk and tying my apron extra tightly over the top. This was it! Despite my nerves, the tiniest flutter of excitement danced in my stomach. I was about to find out what happened at a posh dinner party.

Lord Vye was standing by the drawing-room mantelpiece with a glass in his hand, dressed in evening tails with a white bow-tie. I'd come across him a few times since arriving at the Hall and, while this might sound odd, he struck me as rather airy-fairy, somehow - too insubstantial to be a viscount. You could walk into the room and not even notice he was there. He had wavy light brown hair and kind eyes, and seemed to spend a lot of time painting in his studio (which Gran told me used to be the old servants' hall, in a wing that was mostly shut up).

Her Ladyship was sitting in an armchair on the other side of the fire. Her eyes flickered over me for a second before she rose to greet the Winstanleys. 'Barbara! Reginald! How delightful to see you, and how prompt you are, as always.' An ivory satin evening gown, cut low at the front and with hardly any back at all, swirled around her feet as she walked, and a pearl choker with a diamond clasp circled her slim neck. She had thick, honey-coloured hair set in a Marcel wave and the same grey eyes as Nancy and Julia, but there was something cold and remote about the way she stared at the world down her long elegant nose, head tilted slightly to one side. Gran said it was because she was short-sighted, but then why didn't she just wear spectacles?

Eunice nudged my elbow. 'Ask the lady if she'd like a drink. I'll see to the Major.'

Mrs Winstanley was a dumpy lady in a brown crêpe frock: a dull peahen next to her peacock of a husband in his scarlet hunting coat with shiny gilt buttons. 'A small sherry, please,' she ordered, which was easy enough because the decanter with its name label was waiting next to a tray of glasses on the side table.

I poured the sherry and was about to take it over when Eunice thrust a silver salver me. 'On a tray,' she muttered. 'Nothing by hand.'

That was a close shave; I decided to trail Eunice from now on and take my cue from her. She approached Major Winstanley and hovered by his elbow with a glass of whisky on a tray, waiting for

Isobel's Story

him to notice her when he felt like it, so I did the same with Mrs Winstanley. Eventually she took the sherry without a glance at me and without a pause in her conversation.

'Will you excuse me for one second, Barbara?' Lady Vye asked graciously, and I felt an iron hand in the small of my back as she took me off. When we were a safe distance away, three icy words were whispered into my ear.

'Change your shoes.'

I was wearing brown lace-ups. They were the only shoes I had, apart from a pair of summer sandals, tennis pumps, wellington boots for outside and slippers for indoors, but I couldn't start explaining that to Her Ladyship, could I? So I put down the tray and walked as unobtrusively as possible out of the room, then took to my heels and flew down the hall to the kitchen.

'Good heavens!' Gran clapped a hand to her mouth. 'I clean forgot about your feet.'

'But I haven't anything else! Whatever shall we do?'

'Run upstairs to the linen room and root about in that big wardrobe. You should be able to find something in there. So long as they're black, no one'll notice. Hurry, now! The doorbell's just gone again.'

There were two pairs of black button-strap shoes at the back of the wardrobe: one big and one small. I could never have squeezed into the smalls, so the bigs would have to do. Having fastened them as tightly as possible, I clattered downstairs and back to the drawing room, wondering how many more mistakes I'd be making before the evening was through.

'What did you think of it, then, Isobel?' Eunice asked through a mouthful of meringue. 'Your first taste of high society.'

The dinner party was almost over. Nearly everyone had gone; only Major Winstanley was left in the dining room, smoking and drinking brandy with Lord Vye, while Her Ladyship entertained his wife next door in the drawing room. In the kitchen, we were finishing off the queen's pudding (which wouldn't keep) and waiting for them to leave so that we could wash up the last few glasses, cups and saucers. Mr Huggins was sleeping it off in his little room next to the butler's pantry and Mr Oakes was on duty in the hall, ready to give the Winstanleys back their coats and usher them out into the night.

I wasn't quite sure how to reply to Eunice's question. 'Well, everything seemed very grand - and the food was delicious, everyone said so.' Gran looked gratified. Yet the thing was (although I didn't like to say this for fear of sounding snobby), as far as I could see, the guests didn't quite live up to the dinner. The Dowager Duchess was a strange-looking old woman with droopy ringlets falling into her eyes who hardly said a word all evening and shovelled in her food as though she hadn't eaten for days. Major Winstanley talked about nothing but hunting and sat much too close to the poor lady beside him, breathing all over her with his whisky breath. The businessman Gran had been so sniffy about, a Mr Palmer, had a red face with a fringe of sandy-coloured hair around it, and all *he* could talk about was golf, and the number of houses that had been built in southern England since the war. The only person who looked halfway fun or interesting was Hugo Pennington, Lord Vye's artist friend, known to everyone as Pongo. He must have been the one Lady Vye wanted to impress, because she sat next to him and didn't pay much attention to anyone else.

I got the hang of waiting at table quickly enough, once Eunice had told me the rules. You had to approach with vegetable dishes from the left for the guests to help themselves, and clear away empty plates from the right. Mr Oakes was also meant to top up glasses from the right, but for some reason he seemed reluctant to do this - especially when it came to the ladies.

'Mr Oakes was a liability,' Eunice told Gran. 'He kept standing about, getting in the way, and then he poured wine all over the tablecloth when it came to filling Her Ladyship's glass. I got him outside and told him to look what he was doing, and do you know what he said? The ladies weren't dressed decently and he wouldn't set eyes on them in their nakedness. He didn't go near Lady Vye all evening after that.'

'She won't be best pleased, then,' Gran said. 'Oh, hold on, I think the Winstanleys are off.'

'At last.' Eunice wiped her mouth on a napkin and stood up. 'Nearly there, Isobel. Let's clear away the odds and ends.'

The dining room was full of cigar smoke and empty brandy glasses. Eunice and I loaded up our trays and were about to take them back to the kitchen when she paused for a moment by the folding double doors leading into the drawing room. One of them was open a crack and we could hear voices on the other side. I should probably have gone ahead by myself, but it was too tempting to find out what Lord and Lady Vye thought of the evening, so I stood next to Eunice and put my ear to the gap beside her.

'...thought they'd never go,' His Lordship was saying. 'Every time we have them to dinner I swear it'll be the last. Why do you keep on inviting the old bore, Stella?'

'So he'll get us into the Hunt Ball, of course,' she replied. 'Though whether we'll see any of that lot again after this evening's fiasco is anybody's guess.'

'I thought it went all right.' Lord Vye yawned. 'Jolly good grub, as always. Mrs S is a treasure. I hope poor Huggins is all right.'

Isobel's Story

A snort of exasperation from Her Ladyship. 'You'll have to get rid of the man. He falls apart at the slightest excuse. I simply can't imagine what Pongo thought about Oakes standing in for him, and as for that girl clip-clopping about like a carthorse…' Eunice raised her eyebrows wryly at my gasp; Lady Vye might as well have slapped me across the face. What a mean thing to say, when I'd worked so hard all evening just to help out! 'I tell you, Lionel,' she continued, 'I'm not carrying on like this. Tonight's shambles was the final straw.'

Lord Vye sighed heavily. 'Not this again.'

'We simply haven't the money to run the Hall properly, it's nothing but a millstone round our necks. If you're so determined not to sell, we should simply lock the place up and move into the dower house. Then we could manage with a decent cook-housekeeper and a gardener, and it would be a good excuse for getting rid of the dead wood. Quite apart from Huggins, Mrs S is far too old and set in her ways. She's like some fossil, stuck in the past - won't touch a recipe if it's not one of Mrs Beeton's. And I swear the housemaid reads my letters.'

Now Eunice was outraged, too. 'I like that!' she hissed in my ear. 'So she's been keeping tabs on me, has she? The cheek of it!'

My blood was boiling. How dare Lady Vye call Gran a fossil? If I'd had the nerve, I'd have marched straight into the drawing room and told her what I thought about it.

'It's up to Mrs S to decide when she wants to leave.' There was a stubborn note in Lord Vye's voice. 'And Swallowcliffe is my family home. I won't let it fall to pieces like these houses always do when no one's living in them. Tristan will inherit the estate in his turn when I've gone, and his children after that.'

Lady Vye laughed bitterly. 'At this rate, all he'll have to inherit is a crumbling ruin and a mountain of debts.'

'Say what you like, Stella. You can move out of the Hall if you hate it so much but I won't be coming with you. Now good night.' And we heard him push back the chair.

I walked back to the kitchen in a daze, wishing I'd never been tempted to listen in the first place. Gran had spent most of her life looking after the Vyes. Where would she go if they told her to leave? How would she feel? Swallowcliffe was her home, too; I couldn't imagine her anywhere else. And the thought of such a lovely old house being locked up and left to decay was too sad for words.

Chapter Four

Packed my little suitcase to spend a night with Yvonne last week. Couldn't believe my eyes when she drifted in with an early cup of tea looking as neat as when I had wished her goodnight. 'How do you do it?' I queried. 'Easy,' was Yvonne's lofty reply. 'I always sleep in a Lady Jayne slumber helmet. Haven't you seen their adjustable design, which ties at the back and under the chin as well?'

From a shopping feature in *Miss Modern* magazine, July 1939

THE NEXT MORNING, LADY VYE had an early breakfast alone and set off for London in her own sporty little Aston Martin. She told Mr Huggins she'd be staying for a while with His Lordship's cousin, Phyllis Gordon-Smythe, who had a house in Russell Square.

'So I shall have to talk to His Lordship about the accounts,' Gran said, as we were putting the finishing touches to a bowl of kedgeree. 'Not that I'll get much joy out of him, especially when Mr Pennington's here and all he can think about is painting.'

'If there's been some misunderstanding, I'm sure we can trust Lord Vye to sort it out.' Mr Huggins had appeared in the kitchen, just as though nothing was out of the ordinary. He nodded at me distantly, picked up the chafing dish of sausages and carried it slowly out of the kitchen with great ceremony. As it was a Sunday, he wouldn't be waiting at breakfast: the dishes would be kept warm on hotplates for Lord Vye and his guest to help themselves.

Gran caught my eye. 'We won't mention anything about last night. Just forget it ever happened, for his sake. That's what we usually do.'

I hesitated, wanting to warn her about what I'd overheard but knowing what she'd say about me eavesdropping. 'You don't think the Vyes would ever give him notice to leave, do you?'

'I should certainly hope not!' Gran flushed with indignation. 'Mr Huggins only got the way he is by doing his duty so they could carry on living the high life. Can you imagine what he must have gone through in the war? Shelled all day and night, stuck in some miserable flooded ditch with mud

Isobel's Story

up to his knees and lice in his hair, seeing his pals picked off one after another. He and his sort have given everything for us, and the least we can do is look after them now. Lord Vye knows that very well.'

Now I felt awful. 'I didn't mean –'

'Oh, I mustn't take it out on you,' she said, sitting down at the table. 'You weren't even born then, so how can you possibly understand? The terrible waste of so many fine young men, day after day, month after month ...' She blew her nose and then tucked the hanky back in her sleeve. I could tell she was thinking about her son, Tom, buried out in France. 'And for what? Now it looks like happening all over again, if you can believe such a thing. Well, thank goodness your brothers are too young to be caught up in the fighting, that's the only blessing. And your poor father's safe, God rest his soul. The war did for him, you know.'

'I thought he died of pneumonia?'

'That's what it said on the death certificate, but I bet he'd have pulled through if he hadn't been gassed in the trenches.' She patted my hand. 'My pa died when I was young, too. I know how it feels.'

We hardly ever talk about Dad at home; I suppose it makes Mum too upset. I have to look at photographs to bring back my father's face, although the boys have an old baccy tin which still smells like him. 'Do you remember my dad, Gran?'

I asked her. 'Could you tell me something about him?'

'I will, dearie, but not just now,' she said. 'Come on, off you go for a walk before it starts raining and don't mind me going on. We shall come through, I imagine, one way or another.'

So off I went, wishing she would sometimes talk to me about the things that mattered instead of changing the subject as soon as anything important came up. I was worried for Gran but didn't dare tell her why - and something else was on my mind. Mum's latest letter lay in my coat pocket, marking the place in my book.

10 February 1939

Dear Isobel

Thank you for such a lovely long letter, darling. I'm glad you're enjoying yourself and feeling better every day. I might not recognise you by the time you come home! Hope you're managing to help Gran a little and not getting in the way. The first aid classes sound useful but don't overtire yourself, will you? And don't let that imagination of yours run away with you either.

We're all well here, chugging along much as usual. There's been an outbreak of measles at school

Isobel's Story

and Mrs Jones has a nasty cold. Mr Jones has volunteered as an auxiliary fireman but I shouldn't think he'll be much use - he can't possibly get up a ladder with his knees the way they are. Oh, and they're building an air raid shelter at the corner of Huntington Street. It gives me a funny feeling whenever I walk past, but better safe than sorry. I suppose that's what they're thinking.

Stan and Alfie found a kitten in the back alley last week, you never saw such a funny scrap of a thing. They've named it Ginger (very original!) and feed it on bread and milk. I had to laugh when I heard about your cat. Mrs Jeakes was cook when I was working at the Hall, you know. Get Gran to tell you about her, she had a look that would turn your blood to water

You'll never guess who I ran into the other day - your old teacher, Mrs Vernon. She was ever so pleased to hear you're getting better, and we had quite a chat about you going back to school. She's happy to give you a few extra lessons if you need to catch up before School Certificate this summer. That's good of her, isn't it? We can talk some more about all that when you come home, but I wanted you to start thinking things over now.

We're all looking forward to seeing you soon, darling. The boys keep asking when you'll be back.

Swallowcliffe Hall

Let me know if there's anything you want me to send, and give my love to Gran. Stan and Alfie send theirs, and Ginger says miaow to Mrs Jeakes.

Lots of love, Mum

Mrs Vernon was my English teacher, and English has always been my best subject. The trouble was, I'd missed so many lessons because of the TB that it was going to take ages to catch up in everything else, and I couldn't bear the thought of cramming just yet. Mum obviously wanted me home but I wasn't ready to leave. If only she and the boys could somehow come down to Swallowcliffe instead! London was just too dangerous.

I walked past the vegetable beds where Mr Oakes was weeding cabbages in the wintry sunshine and out into the sculpture garden. It was disgracefully overgrown, according to Gran, but I loved the secret paths winding through tangled undergrowth and the golden-hearted ivy snaking up those crumbling stone figures. You could still make out their features, but in another fifty years the greenery would probably have swallowed them up completely. I wondered if anyone would be walking this way then, and whether they'd even realise the statues were there.

Passing through an archway at the bottom of the garden, I took a track skirting the paddock which used to be a cricket pitch. A skein of geese flew over my head, honking to each other; they were probably heading for the lake, too. There was a boathouse at the far end which I hadn't had time to explore. Gran had told me to keep away from the place because it had been shut up for years and probably wasn't safe, but it looked pretty solid to me. I was going to sit there in the sun and lose myself in the Chalet School: *Kaffe und Kuchen* (coffee and cake, I'd worked out) in the snowy Austrian Tyrol. The boathouse even looked like a mountain chalet, I thought, climbing up the wooden steps. It was raised on posts with a balcony looking out over the water and a jetty underneath for boats to be moored, although its rusty rings lay empty. Only one dilapidated skiff was pulled up on the lake's further shore, with gaping holes in the hull and the seats rotted through. No one would be going out on that in a hurry.

After a couple of hearty shoves the boathouse door swung open and I found myself standing in an echoing, empty room. Tattered check curtains hung at the windows and a threadbare square of carpet covered some of the floorboards. An ancient armchair with its springs hanging out at the bottom and a metal folding chair sat opposite each other in front of me, as though they were holding a conversation. There was a sink in the far corner with a cracked china mug on the draining board - and a dead spider curled up underneath it, I discovered. Somebody must have trapped it there.

Swallowcliffe Hall

I didn't particularly like that place; it smelt damp and sad. The sunny balcony was a much more inviting prospect, so I dragged the folding chair outside and settled myself down, breathing in great lungfuls of healthy fresh air. Gran would be pleased. You could see the south face of the Hall across the lake, and I hoped she'd be sitting in her armchair by the kitchen window. Lord Vye and Mr Pennington were having a painting lunch of soup and sandwiches in the studio, so she ought to have had time for a rest.

Swallowcliffe was so lovely, with its honey-coloured stone and that graceful sweep of garden running down to the water. How could Lady Vye bear to live anywhere else? London seemed drab and dirty in comparison. Streets of houses just the same as each other except for the colour of the front door or pattern of the net curtains, smog so thick you can taste it, and not a glimpse of anything green or beautiful anywhere.

Laying down my book, I walked to the edge of the balcony and leaned out over the mildewed rail, trying to fix the view in my memory. Then a flicker of movement registered in the corner of my eye. Somebody else was looking out over the lake, too. It was the German boy, sitting on a tree stump among tussocks of grass with some kind of paper on his lap. What was he doing there? Not wanting him to see me watching, I stepped back hastily. Too hastily; my foot

Isobel's Story

skidded on the damp wood and I lost my balance. Lurching against the balcony rail, to my horror I felt the rotten wood gave way beneath me with a sickening crack and found myself falling through the air, my coat flying out around me. It happened so quickly, I didn't even have time to scream. As soon as I hit the water, the icy shock of it took my breath away. Gasping and spluttering, I floundered about like some ungainly sea monster beneath the weight of saturated Harris tweed. Drowned by her coat, I thought, struggling in vain to shrug it off. What a way to go.

'Hold on! I help you.' Suddenly I became aware of the boy splashing through the shallows towards me, half-wading, half-swimming, carving a path through the bobbing carpet of waterlilies. He reached me at the precise moment my feet touched the muddy bottom of the lake and I managed to stand. The water came to just above my waist. We stood there, staring at each other.

'Are you all right?' he asked.

'Yes, thank you.' I had to force out the words between chattering teeth. My hair was plastered to my head and foul-smelling pondweed dripped into my eyes; I couldn't remember ever having felt so ridiculous in all my life.

'Come! You must get out at once.' He gave me his hand, but I was too embarrassed to take it. What must I have looked like? It was too awful to imagine.

'Thanks, but I c-can manage.' I started wading for the shore, leaving him to follow behind. It was hard work, leaning into that mass of water with sodden clothes weighing us down, but at last we made it on to dry land. The German boy took off his cap and ruffled his hair, sending a spray of droplets into the air, then wrung out the bottom of his woollen jersey.

'You're s-so wet! I'm sorry,' I said. 'The balcony just g-gave way and I didn't know how d-d-deep the water was.'

'That's all right. I'm glad you are safe.' He held out his hand again. 'Hello. My name is Andreas Rosenfeld.'

'Mine is Isobel, Isobel G-Green.' I nearly laughed, in spite of everything; we might have been introducing ourselves at a tea party. Of course I couldn't think of anything else to say but it didn't matter, not with the state we were both in.

'You must not stand in wet clothes, it is very bad,' said Andreas Rosenfeld.

By now I was shivering uncontrollably. 'I know. N-n-nor should you. Just let me g-g-get my book and we can g-go back to the Hall and change.'

'I will get it for you. That outside place - the balcon, you call it? - is dangerous.' He set off up the boathouse steps while I jigged about from one foot to the other, rubbing my arms and legs to keep the circulation going. The sodden coat lay heavy on my shoulders and rivulets of muddy water trickled down my neck and wrists, dripping on to the ground. Whatever would Gran say when she saw me?

'We must walk fast to keep warm.' Andreas handed me back my book and set off at a smart pace, swerving off course only to collect some kind of sketchbook and a small black tin from the tree stump he'd been sitting on. I struggled to keep up with him, wracking my brains for anything I could possibly say to retrieve some dignity. Nothing came to mind.

By the time we'd marched back to the Hall, some feeling had come back into my limbs. 'Oh, my goodness!' Gran put down the bowl she was holding and hurried over. 'What on earth's happened to you?'

'I had a fall and ended up in the lake,' I told her, not wanting to mention the boathouse and realising - too late - that I should have sworn Andreas to secrecy as well. 'This is Andreas. You know, from Mr Tarver's shop?' Gran must have recognised him as the delivery boy. 'He helped me out.'

'Did he, indeed?' Gran looked him up and down. 'Well, you managed to get yourselves wet enough in the process. Give me your coat, Izzie, and then go upstairs to change. I'll see if Mr Huggins can find some dry clothes for this young man.'

It was wonderful to take off my sopping things, despite the bathroom being in its usual arctic state. I dunked my head in a basin of warm water, washed the worst of the muck off my body with a flannel, and then rubbed my skin back to tingling pink with the rough towel. Looking in the mirror, I could see my hair was the most terrible mess, but at least my eyes were clear and shiny. I have green eyes, from Dad; I wondered in passing whether Andreas had noticed them. Some hope. The only thing he would have noticed was my wonderful impression of the Loch Ness Monster.

There was no sign of him in the kitchen when at last I ventured downstairs with an armful of wet clothes for the laundry hamper. 'Now get this hot soup down you,' Gran said. 'It's not quite dinnertime, but I shouldn't think Mr Huggins will object, given the circumstances.' She handed me a steaming bowl of chicken soup and dumplings, and stared at me suspiciously while I ate it at the kitchen table. 'You didn't arrange to meet that boy out by the lake, did you?'

'No!' I protested. 'I had no idea he was there until I fell in.'

'Well, I wonder what he was - '

I shushed her with a look, because Andreas was suddenly hovering about in the doorway, wearing a pair of baggy trousers held up with a piece of string, a collarless shirt and an old tweed jacket. Gran nodded at him and he came a little way into the room, holding his wet things in a neat bundle with his sketchbook under the other arm. 'Thank you very much for your trouble,' he said stiffly. 'I will return tomorrow the clothes.'

'Take your time,' Gran said. 'They're not in great demand.'

There was an awkward silence. 'So, I shall go - ' Andreas began, just as I said to Gran, 'Maybe Andreas would like some soup?' It seemed awful to be sending him back to Mr Tarver without so much as a hot drink when he'd gone to all that trouble on my account. Why wasn't Gran being more friendly?

'Do they eat chicken soup in your country?' she asked.

Andreas nodded enthusiastically. 'Oh, yes. My mother makes it often.'

Gran ladled out another bowlful while I jumped up to fetch a spoon and lay him a place at the table. Andreas put down his things next to Mrs Jeakes's basket and attempted to stroke her; she hissed at him (as anyone could have told him she would) and shot out of the kitchen like a bullet. He took the soup from Gran and sat down, breathing in the smell of it for a moment with his eyes shut. Something in his expression made Gran and me watch without speaking as he took his first mouthful. In fact, none of us said a word until the bowl was empty.

'Well?' said Gran. 'Is it as good as your mother's?'

Andreas cleared his throat. 'Almost.'

I could tell Gran wasn't pleased, but she should

have been; he was obviously paying her a great compliment. 'It is the best thing I eat in England,' he added, a fraction too late.

'So where exactly have you come from?' I asked. This was one of the questions I had thought up in the bathroom.

'From Berlin, in Germany. I come from there a little before Christmas.'

'Funny time of year to go travelling,' Gran said. 'Were your parents happy about it, sending you over here for Christmas all on your own?'

'There was no time to wait,' Andreas replied. 'And we are Jewish, Christmas is not so important to us. It is just my mother and me, because my father is dead some years.' He straightened his spoon so that it lay exactly in the middle of the bowl. 'Things are very bad for Jews in Germany now. Perhaps you know this? There was a chance for me to come to England, so my mother said, you must go. Then perhaps she can join me.' He looked up at us both. 'Do you think in this house there is work for her? She can do anything. Cook, or clean. Anything you want.'

Gran shook her head. 'There are no vacancies here. Still, if her soup is as good as you say, she should find a place in Germany easily enough.'

'She has to leave there,' Andreas said. 'Please, if you hear of a job, please to tell me.'

'There are plenty of people in this country

Isobel's Story

looking for work.' Gran took away his bowl to wash up. 'We don't need any more from foreign parts.'

'Thank you for the soup,' Andreas said, to her back. 'It was very good.'

I smiled at him to try and make up for Gran's sharpness. 'Thank you for helping me. I hope you won't catch a cold.'

'Now, look here, young man,' Gran said, coming back from the sink. 'I don't know if Mr Huggins has had a word with you, but you shouldn't have been wandering around here on your own. This house and gardens are private property and you were trespassing.'

Andreas drew himself up. 'I am sorry for doing this,' he said. 'I will not come again. But I like to paint, and I made a picture of the lake.'

'Let's see it, then.'

Surely Gran didn't have to be quite so brusque? Andreas was looking more uncomfortable by the minute. He took a piece of paper out of the sketchbook and passed it to Gran without a word. I looked over her shoulder. It was a small watercolour of the same view that had captivated me: across the water to the golden-grey south face of the house, set in a framework of spiky tree branches. Small, but perfect, like an illustration from a fairy tale. I thought it was one of the loveliest things I'd ever seen.

'Very nice, I'm sure,' Gran said, holding it back out to him. 'But you were trespassing all the same.'

'I will not come again,' Andreas repeated. He put the sketchbook back under his arm. 'Please to keep the picture, if the family would like it. Goodbye. And thank you for the soup.'

'Well, cheeky young devil!' Gran exclaimed after he'd left. 'As if Lord Vye would want one of *his* paintings! He's got more than enough of his own.'

'It's wonderful, though.' I took the picture from her hands for another look. 'Don't you think so?'

She sniffed. 'It's all right, I suppose, if you like that sort of thing. But what was that boy up to, snooping around here by himself? There are plenty of other places he could have gone sketching.'

We heard an imperious miaow and Mrs Jeakes came stalking back into the kitchen. 'The cat didn't like him,' Gran added, as if to clinch the matter. 'I've never seen her move so fast.'

But Mrs Jeakes is a fat old tabby with a mean disposition; she doesn't like anyone. That didn't prove a thing, did it? 'It's just as well he *was* there, whatever the reason,' I said, not wanting to let Gran have the last word. 'I might have ended up in trouble otherwise.'

'I suppose that's something to be said for him,' she acknowledged eventually. 'It's just … that voice! Makes me wonder what his father did in the war. What if he was the very man who shot my Tom? It's not easy for someone my age to welcome a German with open arms, in all honesty, and you'll find a lot of people feel the same.'

Which was hard on Andreas, I thought.

Chapter Five

Urgent appeal! Would noble-minded people assist (Jewish) Viennese couple to come to London: capable for every kind of housework: knowledge of English, French and Italian, wife, excellent cook and good dressmaker: both in best health.
Advertisement in the *Jewish Chronicle*, 1938

LORD VYE AND MR PENNINGTON *did* like Andreas's picture, as it turned out, despite Gran's reservations. Mr Huggins was happy to let me collect the dirty plates from their painting luncheon, since it was Sunday afternoon and he had the newspaper to read, so I wrapped the watercolour in tissue paper and smuggled it into the studio under my tray. A risky move, but either His Lordship didn't realise that Andreas must have been roaming around the grounds without permission, or he didn't care.

'I say, this is rather good,' he said, taking the picture over to the window where the light was better. 'Who painted it, did you say?'

'The German boy who's working at the village shop,' I replied hesitantly, knowing that Gran would have had a fit if she could have overheard me. 'His name is Andreas Rosenfeld.'

'Come and take a look at this, Pongo,' His Lordship called to Mr Pennington, who was leaning over the long table where twenty servants used to sit for their meals. That day it was covered in sheets of paper with wispy pencil drawings all over them. Lord Vye was going to paint a mural of Italian country scenes in one of the guest bedrooms, Eunice had told me, and Mr Pennington was there for a week or so to help him plan it out. (At first His Lordship had wanted to decorate the drawing room but Lady Vye had put her foot down over that, which was probably just as well.)

'Not bad at all,' Mr Pennington thought. 'Perhaps you should get in touch with the boy, Lionel - rope him in as an apprentice. German, you say? I wonder what he's doing over here.'

'He told us things were difficult for him in Germany, sir,' I offered, since they both seemed so open and friendly. 'He's Jewish, you see.'

'Dear Lord, is he?' Mr Pennington handed the picture back to Lord Vye. 'Well, I suppose nobody needs to know if he keeps quiet about it. Up to you,

Isobel's Story

Lionel, old man.'

'I'd certainly like to talk to the fellow,' Lord Vye said, gazing at the painting. 'Hard to find anyone in these parts with the slightest clue about art. Wonder whether he's worked in oils?' He glanced over to an easel in a corner of the room, where a murky study of trees in claggy green paint was languishing. Then he turned back to me. 'Next time this Andreas chappy comes up here, ask him to pop along and see me, would you?'

'Yes, sir.' I started loading up the tray with dirty plates and glasses, feeling pleased with myself.

'Fabulous lunch, by the way. My compliments to the cook.' Mr Pennington smiled at me with his twinkly eyes and I sailed out of the room in high spirits.

I didn't see Andreas again for another couple of days. Gran had a word with Lord Vye about the account at Mr Tarver's and he must have settled it in full one way or another because, on the Wednesday, our grocery order was sent up to the Hall as usual - although not till the afternoon, as if to make a point. Returning from a trip to the compost heap, I saw the delivery bicycle propped against the wall by the side door and then Andreas appeared, dark hair curling out under the same baker's boy cap he always seemed to be wearing. I suddenly became very conscious of my faded print apron, and the pigswill bucket in my hand.

Swallowcliffe Hall

He nodded when he saw me. 'Hello, Isobel. I have brought back now the clothes.'

'Thank you. I hope you're all right, after... That you didn't catch a cold or anything, I mean.'

'No, I am fine.' He didn't smile but, then again, he usually looked serious. 'I hope you are not ill, either,' he added, to fill the silence.

I shifted the bucket to my other hand, remembering at last what needed to be said. 'I showed your painting to Lord Vye, Andreas, and he asked if you could go and see him the next time you were here.'

A look of alarm flashed across his face. 'He is not angry with me? I am sorry to make this picture without asking, like your grandmother said.'

I hurried to reassure him. 'No, no - he really liked the painting. He wants to talk to you about art, that's all. You're not in trouble.'

I could see Andreas turning the idea over in his mind. 'Thank you,' he said eventually. 'It is kind of you to do this thing. I will talk to Lord Vye about art, and maybe he can help also my mother. In this big house, surely there is something she can do.' He looked back towards the kitchen. 'Your grandmother is old. She needs someone to help her with cooking, it is not right.'

What could I say? That Gran agreeing to share her kitchen with Mrs Rosenfeld was about as likely as Hitler taking up flower arranging? Anyway, that

Isobel's Story

was beside the point, as I tried to explain. 'The thing is, it is a big house, but the Vyes don't have as much money as you might think. I don't think they can afford to take on anyone else. I'm helping Gran at the moment but they're not paying me.'

Andreas stared at me for a moment without speaking. 'So where is Lord Vye?' he asked, in a flat voice. 'Shall I see him now?'

'He's probably in the studio. The butler will take you there.'

We went back through the blue-painted door to find Mr Huggins - who looked extremely dubious about the idea of Lord Vye showing any interest in Mr Tarver's delivery boy (and a foreigner, to boot) but eventually agreed to go to the studio and ask. I left Andreas waiting outside the butler's pantry, alone in the long empty corridor.

'At last! I was beginning to think we'd have to start the party without you,' Gran said as soon as I reappeared in the kitchen.

While I'd been away, a white lace cloth had been thrown over the table and on it stood the second-best silver tea service, a cake covered in pink and white icing, a plate of bread and butter triangles with a pot of plum jam, and a dish of shortbread biscuits. There was a parcel at my place with a card tucked into the yellow ribbon, and Eunice was sitting there, too.

'Oh, Gran!' I gave her a hug. 'I thought everyone

had forgotten it was my birthday.' I'd turned fifteen that morning.

'As if we would.' She felt in her apron pocket. 'Now there's a card here from your mother, and Sissy will be down shortly with the girls. They've got something for you, too. Eunice, will you be so good as to pour?'

I put Mum's card by my plate to open later in private. This was the first birthday I'd ever spent away from home and I wasn't quite sure how to feel about it. Eunice gave me a postcard with 'Greetings from Bournemouth' above a picture of the seafront and 'Fondest birthday wishes from Eunice Priddy,' written on the back. She toasted me with her teacup. 'Many happy returns, Isobel. Chin chin.'

I opened Gran's card (two fluffy kittens) and then the parcel, which was intriguingly large and soft. Inside were two woollen skirts lined with silk, one a soft pinky grey and the other pale green, and the loveliest dark red crêpe frock with a lace collar. I held the clothes up, one after the other, hardly able to believe my eyes. 'They're beautiful! All for me?'

'Well, you need something else to wear,' Gran said, 'and there wasn't anything else I could do with these old clothes up in the attic. I've altered the frock and remade the skirts but they're good as new. Harris tweed, you see. It lasts for ever.'

Eunice sniffed. 'You wouldn't catch me in someone else's cast-offs.'

Isobel's Story

I held the soft wool up to my face, breathing in a faint scent of mothballs and lavender. It didn't matter in the slightest that some Lady Vye might have worn this tweed before me. The link with Swallowcliffe was what I wanted; it made the clothes even more precious. 'Thank you, Gran. I love them all. You've done a wonderful job.' Her stitches were so tiny as to be almost invisible.

'Let me know if anything doesn't fit,' she said, looking pleased. 'I've tried to leave some room for growth.' Suddenly she caught sight of Andreas's bicycle through the window. 'That German lad's never still here, is he? What on earth can he be up to?'

'I think he might be in the studio with Lord Vye,' I said casually. 'Discussing painting.'

Gran shot me one of her looks. 'I hope you haven't been sticking your oar in where it's not wanted.'

'He's Jewish, you know,' Eunice put in. 'Elsie told me.' (Elsie was her friend in the village, who cleaned for the Murdochs.) 'Mr Tarver's taken him in out of the goodness of his heart, to show him proper Christian ways.'

'He'll be getting his two penn'orth out of the boy in the process, you can be sure of that,' Gran remarked, blowing on her tea to cool it.

'So now he's worming his way in with Lord Vye, is he?' Eunice went on. 'They're like that, Jews, good at feathering their own nests. And once they've got their feet under the table, you'll never - '

Luckily Sissy appeared at that moment with the twins, so that particular conversation had to come to an end. 'Happy birthday,' they chorused, presenting me with their cards. Julia had drawn some kind of large grey animal with a blob on the top, and Nancy, a brown-haired princess in a pink dress. I knew that's what she must have been because both girls loved the two princesses at Buckingham Palace; Sissy saved them photographs of the Royal Family from *Picture Post* and they were forever playing princess games and acting out princess stories. 'Is that Princess Margaret Rose?' I asked her, taking a guess on her favourite, and she nodded with great satisfaction.

'And I've done an elephant,' Julia broke in, 'with a man riding on him. I copied it from the Noah's Ark.'

'Very nice, dearie,' Gran said. 'Now sit down and eat your bread and butter before we cut the cake.'

'We've had such a busy morning.' Sissy plumped herself down in the chair Eunice had pulled out for her. 'Miss Murdoch came up to the nursery. She's teaching you to read, isn't she, girls?'

'I can read already,' Julia said.

'So can I,' Nancy added, although I knew that wasn't strictly true. I'd often read the girls stories at bedtime and, while Julia could follow along with her finger, Nancy wasn't at all interested in making out

Isobel's Story

the letters. It was high time they had lessons from somebody, although Miss Murdoch wouldn't have been my first choice.

'Then she'll have an easy job, won't she?' Gran said. 'Eat up, girls, and we can sing Happy Birthday to Isobel.'

It felt strange, not having Mum and the boys there - as though I had become part of another family. Which in a way was what had happened, I thought to myself, looking around the table. I couldn't go home now, not when everything was beginning to seem so familiar. I didn't even mind doing chores; Gran was teaching me how to cook and it was fun pretending to be a house-parlourmaid, like a dressing-up game. The thought of going back to grimy old London and swotting for School Cert made my heart sink.

When the party was over and Gran had gone upstairs for a rest, I opened Mum's birthday card. She'd sent a ten-shilling postal order, along with two home-made cards from Stan and Alfie and a note: *Have a lovely day, darling - I'm so sorry we're not together. I think perhaps it's time you came home now, don't you? I'll write to Gran and we can make arrangements.*

So that was that, I thought, staring out of the window; my Swallowcliffe adventure would be coming to an end whether I liked it or not. Then I noticed Andreas walking back across the front drive to collect his bicycle and hurried outside to catch him before he left.

Swallowcliffe Hall

'How did it go? Did you have a good chat?'

'Oh, yes,' he said, jerking up the handlebars to turn the bike around. 'We had a very good chat, all about painting.'

'And …?'

'And I will come to his studio again, perhaps, on Sunday when the shop is closed. And we will make some big picture together. The mural, or what he calls it.'

'Well, that's wonderful, isn't it?' He might have looked a bit jollier.

'Painting is not important,' he said, and a muscle twitched in his cheek. 'Why do we talk about pictures at this time?'

'So you asked him about a job for your mother.' My heart sank.

'Of course!' Andreas glared at me. 'If it is your mother, will you not do the same? This big house, so many people can be safe here. But he is not interested. Nobody is interested.' With a sudden movement, he threw down the bicycle and turned to me with his eyes burning. 'That book you read, about the school in Austria?'

'The Chalet School, you mean? Oh, I'm not really reading that, it's far too young for me, I just - '

'Do you know what happens in Austria?' he interrupted. 'It is German now. Hitler's soldiers come and say now this country is ours, you sing Nazi songs and say Heil Hitler and hate Jews like we do.

Isobel's Story

Does your book tell you these things?'

I didn't know what to say. Of course there wasn't anything in *The New Chalet School* about Hitler and the Nazis; it wasn't that sort of book.

'I will tell you about *my* grandmother,' Andreas went on. 'She lived in a special house for old people, old Jewish people. One night the soldiers come and burn the synagogues everywhere in Germany, and break windows and take away the men. *Kristallnacht*, it is known - the night of broken glass. Have you heard of it? On this night, they come in the place where she lives and take outside the old people. The men they pull by their beards. They burn the prayer books in a big fire and say, now clear up the ashes and clean the ground with brushes. Be quick! At first everyone is laughing at the old people, and then they beat them. A man kicks my grandmother so she falls and hits her head on the road, and she dies. Many people die that day.'

It took a few seconds for what he was telling me to sink in. 'I'm sorry.' The words were so inadequate. 'I'm sorry, I didn't know.'

'Well, now you do,' he said, picking up the bicycle without looking at me.

'Is there anything I can do?' I asked, knowing well enough how feeble the question sounded. 'Anything that doesn't cost lots of money?'

He paused for a moment. 'You can talk with people. Say there are children who need somewhere in England to live. Your government lets the children come, but they must come on their own.'

'Without their parents? Surely no one would agree to that.'

'You don't understand! People will do anything to keep safe their children.' Now he was getting cross again. 'There are such bad things happening to Jews every day, awful things, more bad than I can tell you. Men are taken away or killed in the streets. Our neighbour, he shot his wife and himself before the Gestapo could come for them. Everyone is frightened. It is better for the children to go away alone than to stay in Germany.'

'Surely the Nazis can't just go round killing Jewish people! It must be against the law.'

'There are no laws for Jews now,' he said bitterly. 'We must leave our apartment in Berlin because our neighbour says her sister wants it. Everything inside, all our furniture and dishes and clothes, she took them too. We can do nothing because she has papers marked with a swastika and a Nazi policeman there.'

He put one foot on the bicycle pedal. 'Please to think about what I say. It is all true. And when the war comes, it will be too late for Jews in my country. We must do something now.'

Trying to sort out my feelings, I watched him cycle away. What he'd told me was terrible, almost beyond imagining, but what could I do about it, just me on my own? Who could I talk to? The Vyes?

Isobel's Story

Eunice? No one would listen to me. Of course I felt sorry for Andreas, dreadfully sorry, but now he'd made me feel guilty and mean when I'd only been trying to help. I knew exactly what Gran would have said: that I should have minded my own business and not interfered in the first place. Maybe she was right.

Chapter Six

Yes, when the Jewish blood splashes from the knives, things will go twice as well.
From a Hitler Youth Movement song

'TODAY'S COLLECTION IS IN aid of the Lord Baldwin Fund for Refugees.' Reverend Murdoch sounded faintly bored, as usual. He had come to the end of a sermon about ... Actually, what had it been about? I'd been too busy looking at jewels of light scattered across the floor through the stained glass windows and thinking my own thoughts to listen. Lord Vye sat in front of us with Nancy and Julia next to him and Sissy at the end to keep an eye on them; Lady Vye still wasn't back from London. Mr Huggins, Gran and I took up the pew behind, while people from the village filled the rest of the church.

Mr Prior, the butcher, was a church warden so he was always there on Sundays, and I could see Mrs Olds who ran the dairy, and Mr Williams from the garage where we took the wireless batteries to be recharged once a week. Miss Hartcup who taught at the village school was right behind us, warbling through the hymns in a reedy voice that made me want to laugh. And sitting directly opposite across the nave were Mr Tarver and Andreas, who looked sulky.

'We should not forget those unfortunate souls,' Reverend Murdoch went on, 'for whom the evil threatening this country is far closer to home. We must overcome our prejudice to stretch out the hand of Christian charity, as some in this congregation, I am happy to say, have already done.' His eyes had been fixed on the round window at the back of the church but now he dropped them to look directly at Andreas and Mr Tarver, who gave him a satisfied smile in return. Smug as Mrs Jeakes when she's caught a mouse, I thought, before a sharp dig in the ribs from Gran made me sit back in the pew and stop staring.

'There are leaflets about the Lord Baldwin Fund for Refugees at the back of the church,' said Reverend Murdoch. 'Do pick one up and learn more about this worthy organisation. And now we shall sing hymn number sixty-five, "Jesus shall reign, where e'er the sun".'

Swallowcliffe Hall

Gran had given me a threepenny bit for the collection, but I'd cashed Mum's postal order at the post office in Edenvale the day before and there were four shiny half crowns in my purse. I'd spent two of them on a pair of court shoes to go with my new clothes (which had been distracting me during the sermon), but when Mr Prior brought the collection bag to our row during the hymn, I dropped in the other two. Very quickly, so there wasn't time to change my mind.

Despite feeling cross with Andreas, I couldn't stop thinking about what he'd said. Was everyone else apart from me aware of what was going on in Germany? Why weren't we all talking about it? It was shameful to be so ignorant. We took the *News Chronicle* at home but the only newspaper at the Hall was Lord Vye's copy of the *Times,* and that always looked so dull. All I knew about Jews was that some people in England didn't much like them, especially Oswald Mosley and his blackshirts. They'd rampage through the East End, looking for Jews to beat up, and the policemen would march down our street hiding truncheons under their capes when Mosley was speaking on Clapham Common. I had no idea what Jews actually believed - except that surely the Bible didn't play a big part, and neither did the idea of Jesus reigning everywhere. What could Andreas be making of the service?

I wasn't looking to bump into him when it

Isobel's Story

was over, not after our last conversation, but he disappeared straight away while Mr Tarver and the vicar were chatting so there was no chance of us meeting anyway. Rather a waste, as I was wearing the green skirt with a jumper that brought out the colour of my eyes and the new shoes - but of course, he would have more important things on his mind. Besides, I didn't care what he thought of me or my shoes.

'I hope we'll see you at this week's class, Isobel.' Miss Murdoch was hurrying over. 'We shall be tackling shrapnel wounds. Now, where are the girls? I want to talk to His Lordship about the matter of their attending Sunday School.'

Luckily Mr Oakes was already holding open the car door for Nancy and Julia to climb in with Sissy behind their father, so they escaped this ordeal. Poor Mr Huggins didn't get off so lightly: he was waylaid by Mr Tarver, who wanted to know whether a practice air raid drill had been organised up at the Hall yet. 'We shall be holding one in the village on Wednesday at six o'clock,' he said. 'You should come along as an observer. There'll be no time for dummy runs when the bombs start dropping.'

'What a thing to say to Mr Huggins, of all people!' Gran muttered as we started walking back through the village together. 'Mr Tarver never did a thing in the war, anyway. Flat feet, that was the excuse, but he's got no right to start lecturing people who did their bit last time round.'

The sun had come out while we'd been in church but there was a biting wind which made you want to hurry. 'Why are people so hard on the Jews, Gran?' I asked. 'Why does Hitler want to drive them out?'

She huddled deeper into her coat. 'That's a difficult one. Some people go round looking for a target to pick on, I suppose, and Jews stand out because they're different. They're good at making money and getting the upper hand, and no one takes kindly to that.'

'They haven't got the upper hand now, though, have they? Andreas told me his grandmother was killed in the street for being Jewish.'

Gran stopped and stared at me. 'No! That's terrible.' She shook her head. 'All the same, Izzie,' she added a moment later, 'you should take everything he says with a pinch of salt. I'm sure things aren't very pleasant for him at the moment, but I'll bet he's worked out what a softhearted thing you are. I saw half your birthday money going in the collection. Don't get too pally with him, will you? We don't know the lad from Adam. And like they say, there's no smoke without fire.'

I didn't think that was very fair, but there was no point arguing with Gran so I kept my mouth shut. We were quiet for a while and then she said, 'You know your mother thinks it's time for you to

Isobel's Story

go home?'

'Can't I stay a bit longer?' I pleaded. 'If Mum sends me my schoolbooks, I could study here. Please! If I go back after Easter I'll still have the summer term before School Cert.'

Gran laughed. 'Got it all worked out, haven't you? There's no denying I'll be sad to see you go, but I don't know whether Grace will agree to let you stay. She's right, Isobel - your life's in London, not here. You must be missing your friends.'

I shrugged. 'Not really.' The thing was, being ill had made me different. It had been so lonely and quiet in the sanatorium that I'd forgotten how to giggle and lark about. Mary and Vi had visited once after I'd come home, but we couldn't seem to talk like we used to and they hadn't stayed long. No, I was perfectly happy at Swallowcliffe and I knew Gran had come to rely on me. She'd find it hard to manage now without an extra pair of hands to help with the cooking and washing-up. Sometimes visitors came to look at the Hall, too, and I'd show them around and tell them some of the stories Gran had told me about the Vye family.

'When are you going to stop working?' I asked her. 'Don't you want to take things easy for a while?'

'No, I do not! Better to wear out than rust out, that's what my mother always said. Besides, where would I go? And what would happen to the Hall without me? Nobody else could manage the place, for all Her Ladyship's fancy ideas.'

I let the matter drop. Gran would have been devastated if she'd known what Lady Vye had in mind and there was no sense worrying her for nothing. Yet what if I went home and then she were dismissed, all on her own with no one there to help? Mum had to let me stay at the Hall a little longer.

In the end, we decided that Gran would write to Mum and put my case. And then a couple of days later, something happened which made me even more determined not to leave. I was on the way to my room to fetch a cardigan when I heard an unexpected noise coming from the night nursery where Julia and Nancy slept, with a bed in the curtained-off alcove for Sissy. Somebody was crying. I opened the door a crack and looked in, to find Nancy sitting on a high-backed chair with her head in her hands.

'Nancy? What's the matter? Aren't you feeling well?'

'Miss Murdoch says I c-can't sit with Julia any more,' she sobbed, looking up at me through swollen eyes. 'She says Julia helps me too much and I'm not trying.'

Poor little thing! When she took her hands away, I saw a big red letter 'D' on a piece of cardboard hanging around her neck. 'What's this for?' I asked her, picking it up.

'I don't know.' She wiped her nose with the

Isobel's Story

back of her hand. 'But I have to wear it until I can read this book by myself.' *Reading Without Tears* was lying face down underneath her chair.

'Don't worry, we'll look at it together.' I picked up the book and started smoothing out its pages, which were creased and spotted with dirty fingermarks.

'I should like Miss Nancy to make some effort on her own, if you don't mind,' came a voice from the doorway. Miss Murdoch was staring at me coldly through her wire-rimmed spectacles. 'She relies far too heavily on other people as it is.'

'Please stay, Izzie,' Nancy whispered, tugging at my hand, but how could I with Miss Murdoch standing there? There was nothing for it but to hand Nancy the book and leave her to unravel its mysteries by herself. I just hoped she wouldn't find out too soon what that D stood for.

Sissy was down in the kitchen, preparing the twins' luncheon tray. 'Those girls need a firm hand,' she said, when I reported what was going on upstairs, 'especially Miss Nancy. She's too used to relying on her sister.'

Nancy was only six, though, and Miss Murdoch was making her feel stupid when she wasn't. I couldn't see how putting a dunce's badge round her neck was going to help her learn anything.

Eunice had come in for her own dinner. 'Elsie says Miss Murdoch thinks Miss Nancy's a bit ... you know.' She tapped the side of her head and mouthed, 'Backward.'

Now I had to speak up; this was too unfair. 'I'm sure she isn't! You should listen to the stories she and Miss Julia make up together. You've heard them, haven't you, Sissy?'

'Oh, I don't pay any attention to all their goings-on,' she said, picking up the tray. 'Is that everything, Mrs S?'

'Wait a minute,' Gran said. 'Fetch me some strawberry jam from the larder, Izzie, so the girls can have a spoonful on their semolina for a treat. And I think we've heard quite enough from you on the subject of the girls and Miss Murdoch. She knows a great deal more about teaching little children than you do.'

I was about to say that might not have been the case, because I'd helped Alfie learn to read, but the look on Gran's face told me it would be better to keep quiet. I was worried about what would happen to the twins, though, if I wasn't there to help them. Who would take Nancy's side?

The next afternoon, I took Nancy and Julia down to the village, to cheer them up after their morning's ordeal with Miss Murdoch. You'd have thought they'd be desperate for some fresh air and freedom but they walked along with hardly a word, their eyes fixed on the ground, their faces set and serious.

Isobel's Story

'Look!' I pointed into the field beside the drive where a couple of wobbly black-tailed lambs huddled close to their mothers. 'Aren't they sweet? That means winter's nearly over. Tristan will be home for the holidays before long and then it'll be Easter.' If only I could stay until then! Swallowcliffe must look beautiful with all the trees bursting into blossom and flowers everywhere.

'We may not last until Easter,' Julia said, watching one of the lambs begin to feed. 'Our lives are too horrible.'

'Miss Murdoch is sucking all the happiness out of us,' Nancy added. 'She's mean and cruel and she looks like a rabbit. Mixed up with a donkey.'

'Nancy! Don't be rude.' All the same, I could see exactly what she meant and it was hard not to laugh. Miss Murdoch had lank grey-brown hair and a long, droopy face, as though someone had taken hold of her scalp in one hand and her chin in the other and pulled hard in opposite directions.

'Do you know what she did this morning?' Julia asked.

'She put the cover on Punchy's cage and shut him in Tristan's bedroom!' Nancy continued. 'She said he was looking at her in an evil way.'

Punchy was a grey African parrot who lived in the day nursery. He spent the day spitting out seeds and watching proceedings through his round beady eyes, uttering the occasional squawk or exclamation of disgust. 'That will never do, Charles!' was one of his favourite sayings. I was wary of Punchy myself, but the twins were devoted to him and would happily let him perch on their shoulders or heads, his scaly black toes tangled up in their pale hair.

'Miss Murdoch hates living creatures. She'd sooner they were all dead so she could eat them.' Julia folded her arms and glared at the sheep.

'Now that's enough!' They couldn't be allowed to carry on like this. 'If there's one more word from either of you about Miss Murdoch, we'll go straight home.'

There was nobody much about as we approached the shop. A notice was pasted on the door. 'AIR RAID DRILL', it read. 'When you hear the ALARM (rattle operated only by ARP warden), proceed immediately to your shelter or other designated place of safety and remain there until the ALL-CLEAR is sounded (long whistle blast). Do not forget your GAS MASK but do not stop to take any other items with you. CALM and ORDERLY behaviour is essential. PANIC costs LIVES.'

Perhaps it was just as well Nancy couldn't read. I pushed open the door. Would Andreas be there? I found myself disappointed not to see him, although in some ways it was a relief; I wouldn't have known whether to say hello.

'Any word from Lady Vye?' Mr Tarver enquired in a silky voice, passing us a sherbet fountain and two liquorice bootlaces across the counter. 'She's certainly having a nice long visit to London.'

'Her cousin's daughter is being presented at Court in the middle of March,' I replied, repeating what Eunice had told me the day before. 'She'll be back after that.'

'Very good. You girls will be happy to see your mother home, won't you?' Nancy and Julia were not so easily won over; they stared silent and unsmiling at Mr Tarver, hand in hand, as I paid for the sweets.

We were walking back up the road when Andreas came cycling towards us, his cheeks flushed with the cold. I couldn't pretend not to have seen him, he was too close for that, but he obviously wanted to talk and pulled up the bicycle straight away. 'Isobel, I am happy to see you. There is a thing I want to say.'

Now what was he going to lecture me about?

'I am sorry for the last time, the things I said,' he went on. 'It is not your fault what happens, and you have done a good thing for me, to show my picture to Lord Vye. So thank you.'

'That's all right,' I muttered, hating myself for being so mean-minded. 'It's a lovely painting. I'm not surprised he liked it.'

'I will make you another one. Of the boat house, perhaps.'

I snatched a quick look to see whether he was joking. Why did his smile have such an effect on me?

Because he was usually so serious, I suppose. 'I shall come to the Hall on Sunday,' he went on. 'Perhaps you will be there?'

'I hope so. My mother wants me to go back home to London, but we've written asking her to let me stay for a while longer.'

'I am sorry if you go home,' he said, making me blush. 'You are the first person I talk to about such things. I hope we will be friends.'

It was a strange idea; I'd never had a boy for a friend before. Andreas was different, though. I still didn't know what to talk to him about, but somehow there was a connection between us which meant that didn't matter so much. I looked him in the face for the first time. 'If I have to go home, perhaps we could write to each other?' My cheeks were flushing hotter by the minute.

'Yes, and then my English will be better. And you will come again soon, to visit your grandmother?'

Suddenly I was distracted by the fact that both the girls were gazing up at him with rapt attention; they seemed particularly fascinated by his cap. Quickly, I stood in front of them so he wouldn't notice. 'Yes, of course I will. In the summer, perhaps.'

He hesitated, glancing over my shoulder down the lane. 'It is difficult for me with Mr Tarver,' he said, all in a rush. 'In the shop, and the apartment afterwards.'

I could imagine it was. Mr Tarver had rooms

Isobel's Story

above the shop, two narrow windows draped in grimy net curtains looking out on to the street. In a flash, I could picture the awkward meals up there; no conversation, only the ticking of a clock on the mantelpiece to disturb the silence. I'd seen the way Mr Tarver constantly watched Andreas to see if he was pinching anything. What must it feel like to have his eyes fixed on you day and night? And Andreas had no one to talk to except me. How could I not be his friend?

'I want to ask something,' he went on. 'Is Lord Vye a good man?'

The question took me by surprise. 'Well, yes, I think so. As far as I know, anyway. Why do you ask?'

'Because I must live somewhere else. It is not right for me, in the shop all day, and so much church and now Bible study on Sundays as well. Mr Tarver tries to turn me into another person. He wants to save me and I do not have to be saved.'

I remembered his closed, obstinate face in church. 'Does that really matter so much? Couldn't you just go along with it and pretend?' It's what I do most of the time, though I didn't like to say so. Mum's never been much of a one for church-going, and the boys and I fell out of the habit of saying our night-time prayers a long time ago. Sometimes I pray these days, although I think God must know I don't really mean it.

'I am not a very good Jew,' Andreas said slowly,

'but when my grandmother is killed for that, how can I pretend to be something else? How can I turn away from my family? Of course it matters. It matters more than anything.'

I could see that now. 'But what does all this have to do with Lord Vye?'

'Do you think he will let me stay in Swallowcliffe Hall? I do not want money, only food, and I can work in the garden or somewhere else. I work hard and I am honest. Can you tell Lord Vye this?'

With these words, everything changed. So that was it. With a sinking heart, I realised exactly why Andreas wanted me to be his friend: because I was useful. 'Lord Vye doesn't talk to me about that sort of thing,' I replied stiffly. 'Maybe you should tell him yourself on Sunday.'

He might have been puzzled by the change in my voice but I didn't care. 'Come on, girls, time to go.' Nancy and Julia had started messing about with sticks in the swampy stream that trickled along the bottom of the roadside verge, squatting beside it with their two blonde heads close together. Nodding goodbye to Andreas, I rounded them up and we set off for home. How could I have been so stupid? And why did I ever suggest writing to him? I'd made such a fool of myself! He only needed me to ease his way into the Hall, which had probably been his plan all along.

It wasn't until we were nearly back that I

Isobel's Story

thought to ask Nancy, 'Why were you staring at the German boy like that? It was rather rude. You don't still think he's a spy, do you?'

'We wanted to see his horns,' she replied, very matter-of-fact.

'I beg your pardon?'

'He's Jewish,' Julia explained. 'Sissy told us, and she said all Jewish people have horns.'

'That must be why he wears a hat all the time,' Nancy said. 'To cover them up.'

I couldn't be cross with them but, really! What did Sissy think she was doing, filling their heads with such rubbish? I might have seen through Andreas now, but the idea that he could have had horns sprouting out of his head was so ridiculous I didn't know whether to laugh or cry. The twins had to put up with quite a lecture, although I couldn't get them to pay me much attention. They were fidgeting about, preoccupied by something else, and I could tell they weren't listening to a word I said. Looking back, I should have realised they were hatching a plot, but I was feeling too nettled myself to notice.

The next morning, I was busy in the kitchen with Gran when an ear-splitting shriek made us both stop dead in our tracks. 'Heaven preserve us!' she declared. 'What on earth was that?'

Not a 'what', but a 'who': Miss Murdoch. She was up in the nursery, screaming as though Hitler himself was after her.

Chapter Seven

Jack got to the top of the fir tree
But he was dizzy, and he fell and snapped his neck.
So he was killed on the spot.
From *Reading Without Tears*, 1898

I TOOK THE BACK STAIRS two at a time and ran along the corridor to what used to be the day nursery, now the twins' schoolroom. Miss Murdoch was backing out of the door, her hand over her mouth.

'Are you all right, ma'am?' Sissy came hurrying towards her from the other direction. 'Whatever's happened?'

'Wicked children,' Miss Murdoch breathed, her eyes glittering behind their spectacle lenses. 'Savage, ungrateful little heathens! They can stew in their own ignorance from now on, and serve them right. I won't be setting foot in that room again for love nor money.' She brushed past Sissy and lurched down the passage.

'Oh, heavens, what have they done now?' Sissy stared into the schoolroom, but I beat her over the threshold.

At first sight, everything seemed to be much as usual. Punchy sidled up and down his perch, muttering darkly. Since Miss Murdoch's arrival, the rocking horse and dolls' house had been pushed back against the wall to make way for a blackboard, and all the nursery-rhyme pictures around the room had been replaced by alphabet charts and pasteboard mottoes. 'A healthy mind in a healthy body' read one, followed by, 'I don't sniff, Oh no, no, no, I take a handkerchief and blow, blow, blow', and then, oddly enough, 'Vengeance is mine, sayeth the Lord'. Nancy and Julia stood close together beneath these exhortations, trembling with excitement. They were gazing at the round oak table in a corner of the room. I looked at it, too - and gasped. Squatting in the middle was the largest, wartiest, yellowy-browniest toad I had ever seen. It shifted uncomfortably on its plump, damp haunches and stared back at us from under heavy-lidded orange eyes. Sissy screamed from the doorway.

'Poor Mr Toad,' Julia said. 'He's frightened because Miss Murdoch made such a noise when he climbed out of her bag.' She picked the creature up and stroked it tenderly along its knobbly back. I noticed Miss Murdoch's large black handbag on the floor under the table, a packet of cough lozenges and a handkerchief spilling from its open mouth.

'Leave that horrid thing alone and give me the handbag,' Sissy said. 'I'll run after Miss Murdoch and try to calm her down.'

Julia popped the toad in the pocket of her pinafore and gathered up the bag and its contents, which Sissy received at arm's length. 'Ma'am? Wait a minute!' we heard her call as she set off down the corridor.

Nancy grinned at me, sparkling with glee. 'How did the toad get into Miss Murdoch's handbag in the first place?' I asked, finding my tongue at last.

'I suppose he was lost,' she replied. 'The bag must have been open somewhere and he probably thought it was a nice dark cave and crawled in to hide. That's exactly what happened, I should think.'

'Nancy,' I told her sternly, 'stop making up stories. You know how important it is to tell the truth.'

'We found him in the village yesterday,' Julia said, taking the toad out of her pocket and cradling it protectively in her hands. 'When you were talking to the boy. I carried him home in my gas mask case, and then I put him in Miss Murdoch's bag this morning when she wasn't looking. It was all my idea.'

'You'll have to say sorry. Imagine what a shock

Isobel's Story

Miss Murdoch must have had when she opened her handbag! Why ever did you do such a naughty thing?'

'Because we wanted her to run away.' Nancy's lovely grey eyes held mine. 'Just like she did.'

'We're not sorry at all,' Julia added. 'Are we, Nancy?'

'Then you'll have to pretend,' I told them. 'And what happened to your gas mask, Julia, when you put the toad in its case?'

'I hid it in the ditch.'

'We'd better go and fetch it straight away. You can put the poor thing back where you found him at the same time.'

There wasn't much more to be said. I couldn't bring myself to be cross with them because, deep down, I wasn't sorry to see the back of Miss Murdoch either. That night a wonderful dream came floating into my head, just before I fell asleep. Mum would decide she'd had enough of living in London, and she and the boys would come down to Swallowcliffe. She could teach Nancy and Julia and we'd all live happily together, with Stan and Alfie going to the village school and making friends with Tristan in the holidays. And yet I realised this was too far-fetched, even for a dream: Mum would never consent to being a governess. She'd managed to escape from the Hall years ago and wouldn't be coming back in a hurry - not on a permanent basis, anyway.

Swallowcliffe Hall

26 February 1939

Dear Izzie

Gran tells me it's all right with her if you stay on a bit longer, if that's all right with me. I suppose so, darling, if you really think the country air is doing you so much good. Don't get too settled there, though, will you? I'll send down some schoolbooks and then at least you can start studying.

Perhaps it's just as well you're out of London for the time being, with the way things are - anti-aircraft guns in the park and yesterday the sky full of barrage balloons. Some of the scouts are going to act as messenger boys for the ARP and of course Stan was first in the queue to sign up. Mr Jones isn't required by the fire service so he's concentrating on stocking up the house. According to Mrs Jones, he's filled their larder with tins of condensed milk (a job lot from his friend in the market) and is driving her mad.

No more news, really. Ginger caught a mouse yesterday and left its head on the mat. Lovely! The boys send their love, and we'll look forward to seeing you at Easter. Perhaps we could all come down in the holidays to pick you up?

Isobel's Story

Love to Gran and you, of course. Keep well, darling -

Mum

So I'd bought myself a few more weeks at the Hall. I sat on the bed with Mum's letter in my hand, thinking about everything. I thought about how comfortable I was at Swallowcliffe, how safe its sturdy walls made me feel, despite air raid drills in the village and Miss Murdoch going on about poison gas and shrapnel wounds. I thought about Mum's promise that we would stick together if the worst happened, and how it was all that really mattered. When I was in the sanatorium, Mum would come and visit me every weekend. One day she missed the train and visiting hours were over by the time she arrived, but she waved at me through the window until the matron told her to leave and that kept me going for another week. I thought about Andreas, who would be cycling up to the Hall soon to try and make Lord Vye trust him, and about his mother, still in Germany, and then about all the other mothers who were trying to send their children away. Little children, some of them, younger than Julia and Nancy and hardly speaking a word of English. How desperate these parents must have been, to put their trust in complete strangers! It was an amazing act of faith. Despite the terrible things that had happened to them, they still believed that somewhere, human beings could be kind to each other.

I went downstairs to talk to Gran. She was sitting in her chair by the window, darning socks.

'You're right,' she said when I'd finished, taking off her glasses and rubbing her eyes. 'It's been on my mind too. Maybe I shouldn't have been so hard on Mr Tarver's lad. He can't help where he was born, can he? I heard a programme on the wireless the other day about those kiddies coming over from Germany and Czechoslovakia. They put up a crowd of them in a holiday camp on the coast for the winter. With the weather we've had! I shouldn't imagine that was much fun.'

I took a deep breath. 'Do you not think the Vyes might agree to take some children here? There's so much space and I bet the Refugee Fund would help us fix the place up. We could maybe get hold of those beds you had for the wounded soldiers.' The Hall had been used as a hospital during the war; sometimes men came back to visit the place who'd been patients then, and could remember racing on crutches across the lawn.

Gran looked doubtful. 'And who do you think would look after the poor little things? Who's going to cook for them and make their beds and do their washing? Sissy and Eunice? I don't think so.' She patted my hand. 'It's a nice idea, lovie, but it's never going to happen. You won't get Her Ladyship

Isobel's Story

agreeing to fill the house with refugees, not in a month of Sundays. She's got her own children to think of, for one thing. Lord only knows the habits Nancy and Julia would pick up - they're wild enough as it is. And besides, look at the state of the place. Half those spare bedrooms have got mushrooms growing out of the walls.'

'All right, then. What about finding a governess for the girls?' This was my fall-back plan. 'You know that leaflet about Lord Baldwin's Fund for Refugees?' I took it out of my pocket. 'Well, it says here you can offer to employ and train refugees between the ages of sixteen and thirty-five. There's bound to be a person who can speak good English - maybe even someone who's a teacher already!'

Gran put her glasses back on and smoothed out the leaflet. 'That's not such a bad idea,' she admitted after looking at it for a few minutes. 'And she'd probably come cheap, which should please His Lordship. I could have a word with Lady Vye about it when she comes back next week.'

'But, Gran, there's not much time left. As soon as the war starts, no one will be able to go anywhere. Why don't we start making enquiries? You could put the idea to Lord Vye now, couldn't you?'

'Always in such a hurry, you young people,' she grumbled. 'When you get to my age, you'll realise there's no point rushing into things. They've been talking about war since the autumn and nothing's happened yet. I reckon that Hitler's bitten off more than he can chew - he's just looking for a way to back down without losing face.'

She was wrong about this, though, as we were soon to find out. The next Thursday, I was showing a couple round the Hall who'd turned up out of the blue. It was the very day Lady Vye was due back and she hated coming across visitors so this was a risky business, but they'd made a special trip from London to see the house and I couldn't bear to turn them away. A Mr and Mrs Chadwick, they were, and Mr Chadwick was one of those old soldiers who'd stayed at Swallowcliffe when it was a convalescent home during the war. He wasn't that old, really - coming up for fifty, perhaps, with curly brown hair going grey at the sides and very blue eyes.

'Wonderful place,' he said, turning round on his heels as he gazed up at the marble staircase. 'I've never forgotten it.'

'We live in Scotland,' said his wife, 'but we're treating ourselves to a holiday and Ralph was so keen to take me on a trip down memory lane. He used to live not far away, you know. His father was the vicar in a village near by.' She was nice, but she wouldn't stop talking.

'It's a pity my grandmother's having a rest at the moment,' I told them. 'She was housekeeper then and remembers all about the Hall being turned into a hospital. Maybe you could come back another

Isobel's Story

day and see her?'

'Oh, not to worry,' said Mr Chadwick. 'We're heading home on the night train tomorrow.'

'We've been staying at the Ritz,' Mrs Chadwick put in. 'Ralph's just retired from teaching and his uncle's died and left us a nice little windfall so - '

'Now then, Dottie.' Mr Chadwick was obviously used to reining her in. 'I'm sure this young lady doesn't want to hear every detail of our lives. May we take a look at the portraits on the stairs? All the paintings were put away when the house was full of us rowdy soldiers. Do you know, I'd just arrived here when the news came that Lord Vye had been drowned on the *Lusitania*. Terrible thing.' He shook his head. 'I've often wondered what became of his wife. American woman, she was - absolutely charming.'

'She died too, unfortunately,' I told him, leading the way upstairs. 'In the 'flu epidemic after the war. Her husband's brother, Colonel Vye, came to live in the house for a while to look after the boys but he went off to Kenya when the Vyes' older son, Charles, came of age. And then Charles was killed in a motoring accident so his younger brother Lionel inherited the Hall. He's the present Lord Vye.'

'My goodness, the family's had a sad time,' Mrs Chadwick murmured, looking at the portrait of His Lordship's parents. 'And what a handsome couple they were! You'd have thought they had everything.'

'What about Lord Vye's sister?' Mr Chadwick asked. 'She really ran the hospital, you know. Her son helped out, too. Can't remember their name exactly - something beginning with H, I think.'

'Hathaway,' I said. (Gran had taught me well.) 'Yes, Mrs Hathaway lives close by in Edenvale and so does her son. He's the local doctor.' I hadn't met either of them so far. Eunice had told me that Mrs Hathaway wasn't so keen on Lady Vye and wouldn't visit the Hall when she was at home, but Gran said that was rubbish.

'Nice young chap,' said Mr Chadwick, walking up to the top of the stairs. 'I'm glad he made it through.'

'Let's hope he makes it through the next one.' Mrs Chadwick shivered as she followed him. 'Isn't it terrible about Czechoslovakia?'

I would have asked her what she meant, if I hadn't happened to look through the landing window and seen a dreadful sight: Lady Vye's Aston Martin, tearing down the drive. If she ran into the Chadwicks, they'd soon discover this mistress of the house wasn't half as charming as the one before.

'Would you like a cup of tea?' I asked Mrs Chadwick, turning smartly downstairs. 'There are some interesting copper jelly moulds in the kitchen.'

'Good idea,' said Mr Chadwick, taking his wife's arm. 'Come on, Dottie, I'm parched.' He winked at me and I realised he must have seen the car too, and understood we had to hurry. That was good of him. And when he tipped me half a crown at the end of their visit (which stayed a secret from Lady Vye, thank goodness), I liked him even more.

I was just going to tell Gran about the Chadwicks when she switched on the wireless at four o'clock and we heard the news that German troops had marched into Prague. Awful, awful news, it was, because it meant that Mr Chamberlain hadn't sorted out anything at all. Hitler had promised back in September he would leave Czechoslovakia alone if he could have the Sudetenland, but that promise obviously wasn't worth the paper it was written on. He was on the move again.

Chapter Eight

Advice to Refugees

Speak English if you can – if you cannot, do not speak German loudly in public. The English people are a quiet race. They do not like loud talkers and loud conversation in German at this time is at all costs to be avoided. In the same way, avoid gesticulation in public. The English people are unemotional – at any rate on the surface – and anything theatrical or dramatic offends them.

From a leaflet given to refugee children arriving at Dovercourt camp in 1938/9

'THERE IS GOING TO BE A WAR soon, isn't there?' I was determined not to let Gran fob me off. 'How much time do you think we've got? Should I be going home after all? And what about our governess?'

Isobel's Story

She turned away and started to fill the kettle. 'Now don't get yourself into a state. Nothing's going to happen overnight.'

I felt sick with worry, though, and that was before I'd thought about Andreas and how he must be feeling. He must be desperate by now, with his mother still stuck in Germany. Suddenly I felt sorry for him all over again, rather than angry. What did it matter if he was trying to use me? Wouldn't I have done the same, in his shoes? He needed help and maybe I could give it; nothing else mattered. I hadn't seen him for a couple of weeks - not to speak to, anyway. He'd come up to the Hall a few times to paint with Lord Vye but I'd kept out of the way, and when he cycled down the drive with our groceries, I'd stayed upstairs sorting sheets for the linen cupboard. Now, though, it seemed ridiculous to have been so stand-offish. I had to find out how he was.

'I'm just going out for a while,' I said to Gran, jumping up from the table. 'I feel like some fresh air.' With a bit of luck, the shop would still be open by the time I got there.

Miss Hartcup from the village school stood at the counter ahead of me. I liked her; we were often partners in the first aid classes (taking it in turns to be the victim) and I think she found the whole thing as nerve-racking as I did.

'All your children should know exactly where the shelter is,' Mr Tarver was saying to her as he shaped a slab of butter between two paddles. 'Do they, Miss Hartcup? Is every pupil in the school absolutely clear where to go when the siren sounds? You should have a thorough practice every week until it becomes second nature.'

'I don't want to alarm the little ones,' she replied, frowning anxiously. 'Hostilities haven't broken out yet, Mr Tarver.'

'There may be less time than you think, the way things are going.' Slap, slap, slap went the paddles, beating the butter pat into a yellow brick. 'And what happens when we're flooded with evacuees from London? Procedures must be established well in advance or we shall end up in chaos. Chaos leads to panic and panic costs lives.' He stamped a thistle on the butter and wrapped it in a piece of greaseproof paper. 'That comes to one and six altogether.'

She fumbled in her purse. 'I'm sure we're too near the coast to be receiving any evacuees.' Her voice shook from the effort of standing up to him. 'There are no plans of that nature so far as I'm aware, but if I hear of any I'll certainly let you know.'

'There'll be no need for that. I'm in direct communication with ARP headquarters, Miss Hartcup. Not much will get past me, I can assure you of that.'

At that moment Andreas came out of the storeroom with a sack of something or other. He gave a start when he saw me (perhaps I did the

Isobel's Story

same), then nodded when I smiled. It was hopeless: we couldn't say anything important in the shop, not in front of everyone. Still, at least I'd seen him and been a little friendlier. I bought some hairgrips and was about to leave when Mr Tarver said abruptly, 'The lad won't be coming up for any more of these painting sessions. I need him here on Sundays, to take messages and so forth.'

I snatched a quick look at Andreas, who stared back at me impassively. I had no idea what he was thinking. 'All right. I'll tell Mr Huggins and he can let Lord Vye know,' I said, and Mr Tarver nodded.

Painting must have been the only thing Andreas could enjoy. Was that why he had to be stopped from doing it? Mr Tarver had to control everything he did, slap him into shape just like the butter. If only there was something I could have said to show Andreas that I was on his side after all! Instead, I'd fallen into line and kept my mouth shut as usual. I walked back to the Hall feeling a failure. I shouldn't even have gone down to the village in the first place, because Gran needed me in the kitchen now that Lady Vye was home and Master Tristan was arriving the next day for a long weekend break from school. An exeat, they called it.

Tristan was a serious-looking boy, very thin and pale, with spindly legs poking out beneath his uniform shorts and fingernails chewed down to the quick.

'Poor little mite,' Gran said, after she'd treated him to hot chocolate and gingerbread in the kitchen before bed. 'I don't know much about that school he goes off to, but he always comes back looking like a ghost.'

It didn't take Tristan long to cheer up, though. By the time he'd eaten his own weight in toast and Marmite and had a pillow fight with his sisters, he was a different boy. Nancy and Julia had been in fine form since Miss Murdoch left, and our corridor upstairs was soon echoing with shouts of laughter. On the Sunday morning, he offered to show me round the library.

'Nobody ever comes in here apart from me and Father sometimes,' he said, dragging over the wooden steps. 'Half the books are falling to pieces, but there are some good ones if you know where to look.' He climbed up the steps and took out a dusty volume. 'This is an interesting guide to the wild birds of Britain, and the book next to it has exotic species from all over the world like parrots and penguins. We can find out about Punchy, if you like.' He was sweet, but very earnest; I couldn't help wondering what Stan and Alfie would have made of him.

When I came back to the kitchen, there was an elderly lady sitting at the table. 'Here she is,' Gran said as soon as I appeared. 'My grand-daughter. This is Mrs Hathaway, Isobel - His Lordship's aunt.' She caught Mrs Hathaway's eye. 'I still want to call him

Master Lionel when I'm talking to you.' And they both laughed.

'So you're Grace's daughter,' Mrs Hathaway said, gazing into my face as though she wanted to learn something from it. 'Well, that makes me feel old. You don't look a great deal like her, from what I remember. I haven't seen Grace for a good many years.'

'People usually say I take after my father.'

'Ah.' She nodded. 'I heard he died some years ago. I'm so sorry. And how is your mother, dear? Is she happy?'

I didn't know how to answer. 'I suppose so. She likes her job, I think, and she works very hard.'

'Yes, Polly told me she took classes at night school to be a teacher. Well, good for her. I always thought she'd make something of herself. She was quite a firecracker at your age, you know.' Mrs Hathaway looked at me appraisingly. 'Unlike her daughter,' she was probably thinking to herself.

'Not much change there, then,' Gran remarked.

'What our children put us through, eh, Polly?' Mrs Hathaway smiled affectionately. 'Maybe there's still hope for them. That would be quite a fairy story, wouldn't it? You know my Philip never married again.'

Gran pursed her lips and looked at the stove. 'I must get on. This luncheon won't cook itself.'

I had no idea what they were talking about, or

how Gran could be so familiar with Lord Vye's aunt. The confusion must have shown on my face because Mrs Hathaway squeezed my hand and said as she got up from the table, 'Your granny and I are old friends, Isobel, so we don't stand on ceremony. I was about your age when we first met, you know, and Polly not much older.'

I looked at them both. You'd have thought Mrs Hathaway was years younger than Gran - perhaps because she was plumper, and her face less careworn. It struck me that Gran looked dried up and tired, and I wished she didn't have to bother cooking somebody else's Sunday dinner. Was she happy? I didn't know the answer to that question either. She was stubborn, though - stubborn as Mum, in her own way - and wouldn't listen to me telling her to take things easy.

'I'll see you later on, at luncheon,' I told Mrs Hathaway. Eunice was off with a cold so I'd be helping Mr Huggins wait at table.

'All right, dear. We'll pretend we haven't met, shall we? Her Ladyship might not understand.' And she winked at me.

I wanted to ask Gran what Mrs Hathaway had meant about there 'still being hope' for my mum and her Philip, but the look on her face told me to save my breath and the Yorkshire pudding needed to go in the oven so there was soon no time to think about anything else. That day, the children were being

Isobel's Story

allowed to eat with the grown-ups for a special treat. They were on their best behaviour: remembering not to speak unless they were spoken to, sitting up straight and finishing everything on their plates - even the brussel sprouts. The girls were dressed in greeny-blue Liberty silk smocks and looked like matching twin angels.

'So how is school, Tristan?' Mrs Hathaway asked as I was taking away her plate.

He didn't answer straight away, just looked up at her. She had such a kind expression on her face that it must have made him forget himself, because instead of replying that school was going very well, thank you, he said something quite different.

'I hate it.'

'Tristan!' Lady Vye was scandalised.

Mrs Hathaway didn't seem at all put out, though. 'Oh dear,' she said mildly. 'And why is that?'

'Please don't encourage him, Aunt Harriet,' Lady Vye snapped. 'Tristan, if you can't behave you'd better leave the table.'

But now he'd started, he couldn't stop. 'The other boys are horrible.' He blinked rapidly and a red flush burned in each cheek. 'Nobody likes me and they take my books and throw them out of the window. The masters are beastly, too. If you can't do something, they hit you with a cane.'

'Come on, Tris, old man.' Lord Vye frowned across the table. 'Everybody has to put up with a bit of ragging at school, that's what turns you into a man. I was beaten often enough and it never did me any harm.'

Lady Vye laid down her napkin and got up. 'I think we've heard quite enough on this particular topic of conversation, don't you? Time for grown-ups to have coffee in the drawing room and for over-excited children to have a rest.' Her voice was light but a menacing undertone made it impossible to ignore - unless you were desperate. Tristan pushed back his chair and ran around the table to meet her.

'Please don't make me go back there tomorrow, Mummy,' he said, clutching her around the waist. 'I can't bear it. I'll work so hard at my lessons if I can stay at home, I promise!'

'For goodness' sake, control yourself!' she hissed, her face rigid with anger. 'Let go of me this *instant!*' She took hold of his twig-like arms, tore them off her body and pushed him away with such force that he fell down.

Mr Huggins caught my eye and jerked his head to show that I should leave the room. I couldn't wait to go. The sight of that little boy lying weeping on the floor was enough to start me off as well.

'How are they doing?' Sissy was waiting in the kitchen to take the children back upstairs when the meal had finished. 'Is Miss Nancy remembering her manners?'

'The girls are fine but Master Tristan's got

Isobel's Story

himself all upset,' I said, dumping my load of plates in the scullery sink. 'He doesn't want to go back to school.'

'We all have to do things we don't want to sometimes,' Gran said. 'I shouldn't think you and I particularly want to do the washing up, but it's got to be done. That's one of life's hard lessons.'

'But he's really unhappy,' I told her. 'If you'd only seen him!' I couldn't bear to go into details.

'In front of his parents, and Mrs Hathaway?' Sissy asked. 'Oh, Lord! I'd better go and take the children away.'

'I know someone else who's all upset,' Gran said, giving me a shrewd look. 'You're too soft, Izzie, that's your trouble. Master Tristan has to learn to stand on his own two feet and he might as well do it sooner rather than later. He might not be very happy at school, but I shouldn't think it'll kill him. He'll just have to knuckle down like everybody else.'

'Gran, did Mum know Mrs Hathaway's son?' I asked, changing the subject. 'What did she mean about there still being hope for them?'

Her face changed instantly. 'Ask me no questions and I'll tell you no lies. Now let's get on with this washing-up. The sooner we start, the sooner we'll finish.' Of course that answer only made me more curious.

I would probably have wondered about Mum and Dr Hathaway for a good while longer if something hadn't happened which left no room for thinking about anything else. The children had been taken upstairs for a rest after lunch before their walk with Sissy in the afternoon. When she called Tristan, there was no reply, and his room turned out to be empty. He wasn't in the schoolroom or with the twins, or in any of the other bedrooms upstairs.

'Maybe he's rooting around in the attic,' I suggested, when Sissy told us she couldn't find him. 'Don't worry, I'll go and have a look.' I'd discovered all the nooks and crannies up there by now. There were about ten rooms, most of them full of broken furniture, battered trunks and boxes of old *Country Life* magazines - just the right place for a boy to sit and read if he was feeling miserable.

Half an hour later, I'd combed every room, but there was no sign of Tristan. He wasn't in the library either, or anywhere in the old servants' wing, and the cellar door was locked with the key still in Mr Huggins' pantry so he couldn't have gone down there.

'We'd better search for him outside.' Sissy was beginning to look worried. 'I don't want to tell Her Ladyship, but if there's no sign of him by dark we won't have any choice. Oh, the silly boy! Where can he have got to?'

She went to ask Mr Oakes if he'd seen Tristan while the girls and I looked in the greenhouses and the potting shed, then wandered around the gardens near

Isobel's Story

the house. It occurred to me that somebody should check the lake and the boat house, but I couldn't go off there with the twins in tow. Swallowcliffe was so big, that was the problem! There were a million and one places a person could hide - and stay hidden, if he wanted to. At five o'clock, Tristan had missed nursery tea and Mr Huggins decided the Vyes should be informed he was missing.

The hunt began in earnest as dusk was falling. Lord Vye and the menservants went outside with torches, while Lady Vye ordered Sissy and me to comb the house again. When there was still no sign of Tristan by eight, His Lordship rang the police. Three constables and a sergeant turned up within the hour and before long they were joined by a search party from the village; word had gone round that a child had vanished up at the Hall and everybody wanted to help. Lady Vye stood by the drawing-room window, smoking and watching the beams from their torches criss-cross the darkness. What could she have been thinking?

Chapter Nine

My program for educating youth is hard. Weakness must be hammered away. In my castles of the Teutonic Order a youth will grow up before which the world will tremble. I want a brutal, domineering, fearless, cruel youth. Youth must be all that. It must bear pain. There must be nothing weak and gentle about it ...That is how I will create the New Order.
Adolf Hitler, speaking in 1933

ANDREAS WAS AMONG THE villagers in the search party looking for Tristan; I glanced down from one of the upstairs windows and saw him in the lamplight on the terrace beside Mr Tarver. Something made him look up and he spotted me too. He must have managed to slip away somehow because, a few minutes later, I heard footsteps along the corridor

Isobel's Story

and he was knocking on doors to find me. I was surprised he had the nerve to go upstairs in the house, but people were all over the place and this was an emergency, so I suppose he took the chance.

'Isobel! I thought you've gone home until I saw you in the shop.'

'No, I'm here till Easter now. Mum says I can stay a bit longer.' I looked away from him out of the window. We were on our own together and in private. It should have been the perfect opportunity to talk but now everything I'd wanted to say had flown straight out of my head. 'I'm sorry that Mr Tarver won't let you come up here to paint any more,' I offered lamely.

He frowned. 'He doesn't want me to get away, but I will. I must. There is nothing I can do for my mother if I am in the shop.'

'Have you heard from her recently?' I asked.

'There was a letter last week.' He obviously didn't want to tell me any more about it. 'But now it is time to think of the boy. Do you know why he has run away?'

'I think it's because he doesn't want to go back to boarding school tomorrow.'

'And what about the girls, his sisters? Has anyone asked them if they know where he is?'

That seemed like a daft question to me. 'They'd have said by now if they did, wouldn't they?'

He shrugged. 'Not if he asked them to keep

a secret. I think we must talk to them. Look, I have sweets from the shop.' He fished a handful of chews out of his pocket. 'It is all right, I pay for them first.' We both smiled, remembering Nancy.

'But they'll probably be asleep by now. Sissy will be furious if we wake them up.'

'I do not think so, not with all this noise and people everywhere. Come on, we must try. Will you show me where they are?'

It seemed to me that we were wasting precious time, but Andreas was insistent so I took him up to the nursery. The twins weren't asleep; they were kneeling on Nancy's bed in their dressing gowns, staring out of the window with their arms round each other's shoulders. Sissy was being questioned by the police downstairs so there was no one to tell them to settle down.

'Hello, girls,' Andreas said heartily. 'Do you remember me? I bring some things I know you like.' He spread the sweets out on the quilt.

'Can we, Izzy?' Julia asked. 'Is it all right?'

'Just this once,' I said, hoping Sissy wouldn't ever find out. 'And you'll have to brush your teeth again straight afterwards.'

Andreas and I sat down on the bed and we all munched away at the chews for a little while. 'There are many people looking for your brother, aren't there?' Andreas said. 'Everyone is worried.'

Neither of the girls spoke, but Nancy shot her

Isobel's Story

sister a quick look.

'It must not be very nice for him, in the dark,' Andreas went on. 'It is cold, too. I hope he remembered to wear a coat.'

'Oh yes, he did,' Julia said. 'And he has a warm jersey ...' Her voice tailed away as she realised what she'd said.

'How do you know that, Julia?' I asked. 'Did you see him going off somewhere?'

She and Nancy looked at each other again, then down at the quilt.

'Look, you won't get into trouble and neither will he,' I said. 'But we need to find him, quick. Anything could happen out there in the night. He could fall into the lake, or some nasty person might come across him before we do.'

'But we promised not to tell,' Julia whispered to her sister.

'Anyway, there aren't any nasty people on the roof,' Nancy said.

On the roof? On the roof in the pitch dark? My heart turned over. 'Girls, you have to tell us exactly where Tristan is, right this minute,' I said, and something in my voice must have frightened the living daylights out of them, because thank heavens, they did. At one end of the corridor on the floor upstairs was a sash window; if you climbed through it, apparently, you could walk along the roof to a flat space among the chimney pots. That was where he had gone.

'Shouldn't we just tell the police?' I asked Andreas.

'That will take too long,' he replied, heading out of the door. 'And a policeman will make him afraid. I have a torch, so we will go there together.'

'You want me up there as well?'

'The boy does not know me. You must come to show him everything is good.' He looked back at me. 'You will not fall, I will hold your hand.'

Oh, that was all right, then.

He led the way upstairs while I followed, trying not to think about what would happen next. Why couldn't we let somebody else bring Tristan down? The thought occurred to me that Andreas wanted to take all the glory for himself, that was why. He threw up the sash window and shone his torch into the night. 'There it is! See, the path between the chimney stacks?'

'But we don't know where it leads.' I stared out into the black void. 'There might be a sudden drop we can't see, or a dead end, or loose tiles, or anything!'

'If the boy has gone out there, so will we.' He put a hand on my shoulder. 'Isobel, I think you are afraid of being afraid. Bad things do not always happen. The fear is the bad thing you have to beat.' Which I thought was cheeky of him, actually. Even if he was probably right.

Isobel's Story

Then before I could protest, he'd hoisted me up on the window sill. 'You go first and I hold the torch behind you. It is quite safe.'

The next second, I was out on the roof of the Hall, with nothing between me and the huge starry sky above. Andreas put his arm around my waist, gave me a little push, and we set off between the chimney stacks. Do you know, it wasn't so bad? Not once I'd got my bearings. There was one scary moment when I stumbled, but Andreas steadied me straight away, and before long we were stepping out on to a flat space on the roof with a balustrade around one edge.

Tristan was crouching opposite us. The torch beam picked out a white, terrified face, and his reedy voice called out, 'Stop! Don't come any further!'

He'd made a camp for himself with pillows, blankets and an eiderdown at the foot of the largest chimney stack. Goodness knows how long he was planning to stay out there, but it was a good hiding place; we'd never have found him if the girls hadn't told us where he was. The only drawback was that now he was cornered - we were blocking off his escape route and he had nowhere to go. To my horror, he turned to a sloping section of the roof behind him and started scrabbling for a foothold to climb up. It was a wild, hopeless attempt: the tiles were too slippery and the roof was too steep. He'd only managed to shin a few feet before he lost his grip and fell down, rolling helplessly towards the edge.

I started forward but Andreas held me back. 'Leave him! He will be all right.'

Tristan ended up slumped against the balustrade, which was all that protected him from the huge drop below. He clutched one of the stone supports and shouted again, 'Don't come any closer!'

'We won't.' Andreas dropped to his knees and sat down, pulling my arm to make me sit with him. He shone the torch along the ground and whispered, 'Say something nice.'

'Tristan? It's me, Isobel,' I called. 'Don't worry, we're not going to make you do anything you don't want to. We've just come to talk, that's all. This is Andreas, my friend.'

'Go away!' Tristan got to his feet, staggering awkwardly. My stomach lurched - he was so close to the edge of the roof and the balustrade was only waist high - but he made it safely across to his encampment and crawled in among the pillows and blankets. 'I'm not going back to school, whatever you say.'

'It is a funny thing,' Andreas said conversationally. 'You hate your school and do not want to go there, and with me it is different. I liked my school very much but they will not have me there.'

'Why not?' Tristan sounded interested in spite

Isobel's Story

of himself.

'Because I am Jewish. In Germany now there is a rule that Jews cannot go to school with other children, they must be teached by themselves.'

'Why do they say that?'

'It is hard to explain. Some people think all the bad things are because of the Jews, so they must stay on their own.'

In the shadows, I saw Tristan sit up on his heels. 'But that's just what I want - to be left alone at home. Didn't you like it?'

'Not so much. There was a very good art teacher at my school and that was why I wanted to stay there, even when things were hard.'

'How were they hard?'

'For two years, the other boys fight with me every day. There was one other Jewish boy in my class and each morning they wait for us, before school and later in the playground. Then one day, we had a good idea.' Andreas was talking more quietly now, and Tristan edged forward to hear. 'We went to the headmaster and said, "Everyone hits us and calls us dirty, lying Jews." And do you know what this man replied? He said, "Well, what do you want me to do about it? That is exactly what you are." So we knew nobody would help us.'

'Did you tell your parents? What did they say?'

'Every day my mother saw my cuts and bruises, but she can do nothing. I did not want her to worry.'

'I have bruises, too.' Tristan shuffled further forward and lifted up his jersey, although it was too dark for us to see anything.

'Then you understand. There is hurt on the outside but the hurt inside is worse, I think. My mother told me a thing about this. She said if a person hits you for nothing, he is the weak one, not you.'

'Did you cry when those boys hit you?' Tristan asked.

'At first, yes, but I learned how to stop. It is not so hard. And sometimes I tried to fight back. I can teach you, if you want.'

'It doesn't matter. I'm not going back there, anyway.'

'Then do you know what those boys will say? They will say, we have beaten Tristan for sure, we are stronger than he is. And they will choose another person to hit next.'

'I don't care. At least it won't be me.'

'But you cannot run away for ever, it is not a good thing to do. You must choose: a boy who runs away, or a boy who is not frightened inside.'

'You ran away, though,' Tristan said. 'You're here, not in Germany any more. Why didn't you stay and stand up to those other boys?'

Andreas didn't reply straight away. Then he said quietly, 'Because it was not only the other boys. It was everyone. Every shopkeeper, every policeman,

Isobel's Story

every neighbour, every person on the street, every friend from before who was not Jewish. I could not stand up to all of them. But you see, now I know it is bad to run away. You must stay if you can.'

Tristan looked at him for what seemed an age. 'Will you promise to help me?'

'Of course I will. We will help each other.' Andreas held out his hand.

'All right then.' Tristan edged forward to grasp it, and a wave of relief made me lightheaded.

We walked back along the roof with Tristan sandwiched between us. 'Andreas,' I said when we were safely through the window and back in the house - but then I didn't know how to carry on. What was there to say, after what he'd just told us? I gave him a quick hug instead, surprising myself.

It was a mistake; he didn't hug me back. 'It's all right,' he said. 'You don't have to be sad for me. Shall you take downstairs the boy?'

'No, you do it. You were the one who found him, after all.'

So Andreas was the one who reunited Tristan with his parents. Lord Vye insisted he stay for supper, and there wasn't much Mr Tarver could do or say about it. I saw the shopkeeper's face, though, and you could tell he was apoplectic about having to go back to the village on his own. He must have suspected his delivery lad would try to change jobs, and with good reason. The next morning, Andreas turned up at the Hall with his suitcase, to start working with Mr Oakes as garden boy. He would sleep in a little room next to Lord Vye's studio (the old butler's pantry) and take his meals in the kitchen with us.

Eunice was scandalised when she heard the news first thing. 'So the shop isn't good enough for him,' she said, coming into the kitchen with her coat half off. 'After everything Mr Tarver's done! You'd think he'd show some gratitude, wouldn't you? I suppose he's wangled his way in here because he thinks this is where the money is. Well, he's in for a disappointment.'

'He doesn't care about money,' I said, 'and he's worked his socks off for Mr Tarver. Why shouldn't he go somewhere else if he wants to?'

'Isobel! That's quite enough,' Gran said sharply. 'When all's said and done, Mr Tarver took the lad in. Still, Eunice, I should say he's paid his dues by now. He was the one who brought Master Tristan back safe and sound, don't forget. I hope we'll all make him feel welcome.'

Eunice gave a little snort at this and tossed her head. 'We shall have another foreign visitor soon,' Gran went on. 'A letter came from the Refugee Committee this morning. They've found a young Polish lady to be a governess for the girls. She sounds very suitable.' And she gave Eunice a look, as though daring her to object.

Eunice left the room without another word,

Isobel's Story

back to the cloakroom to hang up her coat and hat, and Gran went off to sort out the linen hamper before I could ask her anything about the new governess. I was washing up the breakfast plates when Eunice came back into the kitchen, tying her apron strings. 'Dear Lord! As if one wasn't enough,' she muttered to herself.

Alina Lukowski, that was the Polish girl's name. She was nineteen, and she could play the piano and the violin, and speak four languages. According to the Refugee Committee, she had taught at a Jewish school in Warsaw until it had been closed down by the authorities the year before. 'She can have that room next to yours, Izzie, at the end of the corridor,' Gran said at supper that evening. We were all sitting round the table: Mr Huggins, Gran, Sissy, me - and Andreas, wearing an old cotton workshirt and corduroy trousers. (Mr Oakes lived in the gate lodge so he went home in the evenings, like Eunice.) He didn't say much but watched us intently, ready to help when required. Sissy kept shooting him sideways glances when she thought he wasn't looking. Perhaps she still believed he had horns.

Alina Lukowski. I tried her name out in my head, savouring the rhythm of it. Perhaps we'd become friends, even though she was older than me and I wouldn't be at Swallowcliffe for much longer. I could ask her all about life in Poland and she might even write to me when I went back to London.

Suddenly I couldn't wait for her to arrive.

'I didn't realise the matter had been arranged,' said Mr Huggins, wiping his mouth carefully on a white linen napkin. 'That was very quick.'

'No point in hanging about, not with the way things are.' Gran nodded at me to start clearing away our plates and bring the bowls for pudding. 'I discussed it with Lord Vye when Her Ladyship was away. I should think she'll be delighted we've found such a clever girl.'

'And how was your first day at the Hall?' Mr Huggins asked Andreas. 'Mr Oakes keeping you busy, I trust?'

'Oh yes. There is a lot to do, digging and planting potatoes. But I like this work,' he added hastily. 'It is good to be outside.'

'What will Mr Tarver do without you?' Sissy asked. 'It's a bit hard on him, isn't it? You upping sticks and leaving all of a sudden.'

'I think he will be all right,' Andreas said. 'There was nobody to help in the shop before me, but sometimes a boy from the village.'

I shivered inside. Mr Tarver would be furious; it didn't bear thinking about what he'd be saying to all his customers. Still, at least Andreas had got away from him. That was the main thing. 'I will help you,' he said to me, taking Sissy's plate and stacking it neatly under his own before jumping up from the table so promptly we nearly collided.

Isobel's Story

'Isobel can manage,' Gran told him. 'You save your efforts for the garden.'

It would take some getting used to, having him so close at hand. I was all fingers and thumbs at the dinner table, feeling the intensity of his stare, and didn't eat much. It was exciting, though: catching the odd glimpse of him through the window and thinking that now we might have a chance to get to know each other.

Somebody else in the house felt very differently, however. Eunice came straight into the kitchen early the next morning, still wearing her hat and an aggrieved expression underneath it. 'I'm handing in my notice, Mrs S,' she said, without further ado. Her arms were folded across her chest as if to keep in the emotion bubbling up inside. 'You can't expect me to work with a load of foreigners, and Jews at that - it's just not fair. There'll be trouble, you mark my words. Things will go missing and we'll end up getting the blame. They should stick with their own kind, go to London or some other place where there's plenty of that sort already. It's not right for them to come down here.'

I looked at Gran, wondering how she'd react. All she said was, 'I take it you've thought this over?'

'Yes. I'll work till the end of the week and then I shall be off. There's a week's holiday owing to me, if you remember.' And she marched self-righteously out.

Gran sighed. 'Well, I can't say I'm surprised. Sissy'll be next, I shouldn't wonder, and then what will we do?' She put a clean towel into my arms. 'Take this to the lad's room, will you? I forgot to give it him yesterday and now there's Her Ladyship ringing for me.' Up on the wall, the drawing-room bell was jangling so furiously it practically jumped off the board.

Eunice really was a piece of work. What harm was Andreas doing anybody, least of all her? She knew nothing about him, I thought, walking down the passage past the studio and then knocking on the door of the bedroom next to it, even though he'd been outside at work for a good hour. Of course there was no reply, so I pushed it open and went inside. The room was small and on the dark side, but the rich wood panelling made it seem cosy. There was a neatly-made bed in one corner and a chest of drawers in the other with a washbasin on the wall between them, and that was about it. A suitcase had been pushed under the bed next to a pair of black polished shoes and I could see the folded edge of Andreas's pyjamas peeping out from under the pillow, but otherwise there was hardly any sign of him at all. I looked around, not knowing what I'd expected to find but disappointed all the same that it wasn't there.

Then quietly, furtively, knowing it was wrong but not able to stop myself, I started to pull out

Isobel's Story

each drawer of the chest in turn. In the bottom one, nestled in the sleeves of a jumper, I found a sheaf of letters, an envelope full of photographs, and a silver knife, fork and spoon, engraved on the handles with the initial 'R' and some sort of crest. Of course I'd never have read the letters (anyway they were all in German), but I couldn't resist sitting on the bed and looking through the photographs. Andreas at six or so with chubby cheeks and a broad grin, a cross-looking rabbit clutched to his chest; a formal studio portrait of the family, Andreas as a baby on his mother's lap with his father standing proudly behind, one arm resting on her shoulder; a more recent picture of his mother, too, looking much older, and one of the apartment building where they must have lived in Berlin; the view over a lake with mountains in the background, and then the picture of a girl, smiling into the camera, her dark hair wound in plaits around her head. Who was she? I found the picture unsettling for some reason - perhaps because she was about my age, and looked so happy.

I must have stared at the photographs for quite a while before coming to my senses and cramming them back into the envelope, thoroughly ashamed of myself. I smoothed down the blanket on which I'd been sitting, laid the towel on the end of the bed and hurried back to the kitchen. By the time Gran came in, I was innocently drying up the breakfast plates.

'Is something wrong?' I asked, seeing the preoccupied look on her face and instantly afraid of what Lady Vye might have said.

'You could say so.' She sat down heavily at the table. 'Her Ladyship won't hear of a foreign governess, she says she'll be giving the children funny ideas. I've to tell the Refugee Committee there's no vacancy after all.'

"We can't stop her coming, not now!' I protested. Alina Lukowski was a real person with a name and a history, not just a statistic. We'd offered her a chance; it was too cruel to turn around now and snatch it away. Anyway, how could Lady Vye object to a governess who spoke four languages without even seeing her, just because she was Polish? Or Jewish? Perhaps that was the problem. I seemed to remember Sissy telling me the children had had a French nursery maid before her.

'I'm getting too old for all these shenanigans,' Gran grumbled. 'First Eunice handing in her notice - and who knows where we'll find another housemaid - now this.'

I thought quickly. 'Maybe you can say it's too late, that Alina's already on her way.'

'And then what will happen? She'll be sent away with a flea in her ear as soon as she arrives.'

'But at least she'll be in this country! If there's no job waiting for her here, she'll never get out of

Isobel's Story

Poland.'

Gran threw up her hands. 'What can I do? Lady Vye won't have the girl in the house under any circumstances, and that's that. I'll have to write to the Refugee Committee and ask them not to send her after all.' She looked up at the clock. 'Tell Mr Huggins not to take the post till I've finished, will you, dear? He should be in the pantry.'

Letters to be sent waited on a silver tray in the hall; after breakfast, Mr Huggins stamped them and took them down to the village post box. I didn't tell him to wait for this one, but luckily that morning he was behind with the post anyway and the letters were still waiting for him on the hall table when I scurried past, shortly after Gran. It was just as well she hated using the telephone, I thought, slipping the envelope addressed to the Jewish Refugee Committee into my pocket. Let's see if Lady Vye really had the heart to send Alina away once she was actually here.

Chapter Ten

Advice to Refugees

The English people have freely and liberally given you a place of refuge. Show them by your courtesy to others, your consideration for all people, your kindness, that they have been justified in their generosity.

From a leaflet given to refugee children arriving at Dovercourt camp in 1938/9

'WHAT IS WRONG? Is there some mistake? I don't understand.' Alina Lukowski looked anxiously at each of us in turn. 'I wait at the station but nobody came and a man told me to take the bus. Do you not expect me?' She rubbed her forehead with trembling fingers.

'There's been a mix-up,' Gran said, frowning.

Isobel's Story

'I'm sorry, dear, but there's no vacancy for a governess here after all. I wrote to the Refugee Committee - they should have told you not to come.'

'So what am I to do?' Alina sounded on the verge of panic. 'I have no more money for the train. Where will I go?'

'Sit yourself down.' Gran pulled out a chair. 'We'll soon get everything sorted out, don't you worry. Take off your coat and catch your breath for a minute.'

'Surely now Alina's here, she could go and see Lady Vye?' I asked, smiling at our guest to show her I thought everything was going to turn out all right.

Gran drew me to one side. 'There's no point,' she whispered. 'You know what Her Ladyship's like. She'll send the poor girl packing quicker than you can say knife. Oh, what a mess! What on earth are we to do with the girl?'

I felt a knot of panic gnaw at my stomach; maybe my wonderful idea wasn't quite so wonderful after all. And then it suddenly struck me. 'Why don't I put the kettle on?' I said brightly. 'We might as well have a cup of tea.' And I beckoned Gran into the scullery for another furtive conversation.

'Eunice is leaving tomorrow, isn't she? And you still haven't found anyone else. Maybe Alina could be the new housemaid!'

'But Lady Vye doesn't want any more foreigners, she told me that in no uncertain terms.'

Gran was losing patience. 'This isn't some daft plan of yours, is it?' she added suspiciously.

'What if she never finds out Alina's Polish? You can't tell just by looking at her.' Alina had a smooth, oval face framed by light brown hair cut in a bob: almost English-looking. Something about her clothes was subtly different - the cut of her heavy overcoat, the narrow buckles on her shoes, the shape of her brown felt hat - but once she put on an apron, she'd look just like anyone else.

'You can tell as soon as she opens her mouth,' Gran said. 'She might speak English all right but she's got a funny accent.'

'But Lady Vye won't ever speak to her!' I hissed. 'How often does she talk to Eunice? The most Alina would ever have to say is "Yes, ma'am" and 'No, ma'am" once in a blue moon. Come on, Gran, it's worth a try. What else are we going to do?'

'I don't know what the girl would say. Who ever heard of a housemaid who could speak four languages and play the piano?'

I glanced back through the scullery doorway to where Alina was sitting at the kitchen table, her back slumped and her head propped up on one elbow. Tiredness and defeat came oozing out of her in great waves. 'We can always put it to her. If she's desperate enough, she'll agree.'

'What shall a house-parlourmaid do?' Alina asked, after we'd explained the situation.

Isobel's Story

'It's cleaning, mostly,' Gran told her. 'Make the beds, change the linen on Fridays, tidy and dust the bedrooms, mop the bathrooms, vacuum and clean downstairs. Wait at table now and then if the Vyes are having company.'

'This whole big house? Only me, alone?'

We told her that most of the house wasn't lived in, only a few of the bedrooms and bathrooms upstairs being used (Sissy looked after the children's rooms while we cleaned our own) and downstairs, mainly the drawing room, the breakfast room and the dining room. Gran liked to mop the kitchen floor herself, not trusting Eunice to make a proper job of it.

'All right,' Alina said bleakly at last. 'I will do it.' Because really, what option did she have?

'You think she must be grateful. Look at this good thing you have done for her and she does not even say thank you.' Andreas held up a pencil at arm's length and squinted along it, marking off some measurement with his thumbnail which he checked against the drawing on his lap. It was a lovely spring afternoon and the Hall lay spread out below us in the sunshine. Alina had been part of the household for a couple of weeks by now, Gran having introduced her to Lady Vye as the new house-parlourmaid, Angela Lucas. We didn't know what she thought about the position - then again, we didn't really know what she thought about anything.

'Shouldn't imagine you'll get much work out of that one,' Eunice had said with some satisfaction, pulling on her gloves for the last time. 'Looks like a puff of wind would blow her away. Well, goodbye, Isobel.' She'd pinched my cheek with her hard leather fingers - affectionately, I hoped. 'Look after your granny, won't you? Don't let them take advantage.' There was no need to ask who she meant by 'them'.

That night, I'd lain in my bed and listened to Alina sobbing in hers on the other side of the wall until I couldn't bear it any longer and crept into her room. 'Are you all right?' I whispered. 'Do you want to come in with me for a bit?' But she'd only turned her face to the wall and shrugged my hand off her shoulder. Eunice was wrong about one thing, though - we soon discovered that Alina could work for hours. She was a neat and methodical housework machine, going about the duties that used to be Eunice's. And all the time, she hardly spoke a word.

'She doesn't have to thank us,' I said, stung by Andreas's remark. 'I just wish she'd talk to me.'

'You cannot wish anything from her.' He looked up from the drawing with an expression in his dark eyes that was hard to understand. 'Perhaps you think, oh, if this was me I will be so happy to have a friend who helps me in this country. But she is different than you. English people have saved her life but she cannot be your friend so quick. She

Isobel's Story

thinks about things you do not know.'

'Then tell me! I want to find out.'

He sighed and laid down the sliver of charcoal. 'All right, I will try. First, she thinks every minute about her family in Poland, how she can get them out of there. Perhaps they say to her, now, Alina, you must find a way for us to come to England too, ask the good people you meet for help. But everyone has done so much already, she cannot ask for more. She knows she has always to be grateful and that is hard. And then she thinks, why do I escape, when so many stay behind? I do not know the word for that.'

'Guilty,' I said, feeling the very same thing myself.

'Yes, she is always guilty. Like me. The other Jewish boy at school, Hans, and my cousin - and my mother, for sure - I think about them all the time. What happens to them now? And then perhaps Alina does not want to leave Poland but her parents said she must. They have sent her away, she thinks. Do they really love her? Or perhaps she has a boyfriend and she is afraid he will die.'

'Why won't Alina talk to you about all of this, though?' I asked.

'We are both Jews but I am not so religious as she is. And I am German, she hates me for that.' He started to sketch the winding curve of the drive. 'She is not like one of your friends. You know the basket in Mr Tarver's shop with the sign of "damaged goods"? This is Alina and me. We are damaged goods, not nice like ordinary people.'

I watched the children playing hide and seek in the trees around us, thinking this over. Tristan was home for the Easter holidays at last and I'd taken him and the girls up to the Fairview Tower, about a mile from the house through the gardens and up a hill between an avenue of oaks. It was one of Gran's favourite places, although she probably couldn't climb up there now. We'd found Andreas sitting on the bench at the foot of the tower, sketching. I wasn't surprised to see him because it was one of his favourite spots, too; in fact I'd been hoping he'd be there.

Somehow we'd fallen into becoming friends. One Sunday afternoon when no one else was around, I'd seen him working in the greenhouse and plucked up the courage to in and talk. It was shortly before Alina was due to arrive, and I'd been wanting to ask him for ages exactly how he'd managed to escape from Germany. He told me his mother had found out about a programme of trains taking Jewish children to England - the *Kindertransporte*, it was called - and pulled every string she could until his name was down on the list. 'Every day she comes to the office until they say they will take me, and my cousin, Gisela, too. But in the end I am on the train and Gisela is not. She has a problem with the passport or something.' His cousin was fifteen, he

Isobel's Story

told me, and loved ballet and horse-riding lessons. She was probably the girl in the photograph, though of course I didn't admit to having looked at it.

'She can still come though, can't she, when it's sorted out?'

He sighed. 'There are so many now who try to leave, I don't know when she has another chance.'

'It must have been awful, saying goodbye to everyone.' I tried to imagine.

'This was so strange, I cannot tell you.' He was putting seedlings into pots, carefully firming the compost around their fragile stems. Now he paused for a moment, gazing out of the greenhouse window. 'The train leaves in the middle of the night, so it was dark. The parents must wait behind a gate, the Nazis have said they cannot cry or make any noise. They watch as the children get on the train. Many of the children are younger than me, and excited, waving like this is a ... what is the word? An adventure. The parents watch and don't move, like they are made of stone. Suddenly a man breaks through and runs on to the platform, and I think the guards must shoot him but they don't. The train is leaving and out through the window he pulls his little girl.'

'He couldn't bear to let her go?'

Andreas nodded. 'And I wished I had a father who would come and pull me off that train, more than I ever wished anything in the world.'

'You mother was braver than that, though,' I

said. 'She was thinking of you, not herself.'

He gave me a searching look. 'That is right, you understand.' Neither of us spoke for a while, then he hunched his shoulders and let them drop in a shrug of despair. 'But come, we will talk of other things.' And he started to tell me about happier times before his father died: visits to his uncle and aunt in the country, trips to the theatre in Berlin, shopping at the market and buying bread from the baker at the end of their street. 'Good dark German bread, not like English cotton wool.' He smiled to let me know he was teasing. 'And now it is your turn. Say some of the things when you were a little girl.'

So I told him about picnics with my brothers on Clapham Common and the big bonfire on Guy Fawkes' night, about going to the cinema on Saturday mornings, and the seaside holiday we'd had in Clacton before Alfie was born and my father became sick. I told him about having to creep round the house when Dad was really bad, and about falling ill myself and having to go to the sanatorium - even about thinking that maybe I was going to die too, which I'd never told anyone before, not even Mary and Vi. He didn't say very much, just nodded from time to time to show he was listening. I could have stayed for hours in that snug greenhouse, sitting on the floor with my arms wrapped around my knees; by the time I eventually emerged, it felt as though we knew each other properly at last.

Isobel's Story

Just before I had to leave. The next day was Good Friday: Mum and the boys would be arriving in the afternoon and then we'd be going home together on Easter Monday. 'Would you let me have that picture?' I said now, looking over Andreas's shoulder at the sketchpad.

'No,' he replied, and I was blushing for having asked when he added, 'I make you a better one. But you will come back, won't you, in the summer?'

'I hope so.' Who knew what would be happening by then? The war was bound to have broken out and we'd probably be stuck in London, spending the nights in a dingy air raid shelter on the corner of Huntington Street. Worse than that, I'd be going back without having done a single thing to help Andreas get his mother, his cousin or anyone else out of Germany. All right, I'd talked to Miss Hartcup one day after first aid class, but she had no money or jobs up her sleeve and wasn't very keen on sharing her home with a young Jewish refugee. I suppose she had enough of children during the day. What else could I have done? There had to be something.

'Izzie! At last.' Mum gathered me up in a hug. I breathed in the familiar smell of Pond's cold cream and Bronnley lemon soap and realised how much I'd missed her. She drew back to smile at me. 'Well, look at the roses in your cheeks. You've turned into a proper country girl.'

Oh, it was good to see her - and my brothers, too. I'd been waiting at the gate lodge for what seemed hours until the bus from Hardingbridge drew up and the three of them tumbled off. Stan stared around suspiciously. 'So where's the house? Looks like we've been dumped in the middle of nowhere.'

All the little kids in our street love Stan because he looks tough, with his bristly dark hair, but underneath he's a softie who'll play with them for hours. Going away anywhere usually makes him nervous until he knows what's what. Alfie has blond curls and a lisp, but he's much more of a tearaway. Give him an inch and he'll take a mile, that's what Mum says.

'Why's it so quiet?' Alfie asked. 'Where is everyone? And what are those sheep doing in that field?'

'Being sheep, I suppose.' I'd become so familiar with everything at Swallowcliffe that it was funny to see the bewilderment on their faces. I picked up Mum's carpet bag. 'Come on, Gran's made Chelsea buns for tea.'

'Just a minute.' Mum was peering into the windows of the gate lodge. 'I was brought up in this house. Let me have a quick look, at least.'

Mr Oakes and his wife lived there now, though, and Mrs Oakes was a battleaxe so I thought it safer to hurry Mum away. We walked up the drive, the

Isobel's Story

boys kicking a football back and forth across the grass between them. As soon as we rounded the corner and they saw the Hall, the football dribbled to a standstill by itself. 'Crikey,' breathed Stan. 'Are we really going to stay in that?'

'It's not so grand close up,' I told them. 'Especially not our part of the house.' The boys would be sleeping on mattresses in my room, and we'd made up a bed for Mum in a spare room at the end of our corridor, next to Tristan's.

'All the same, you'd better behave yourselves,' Mum said. 'There's to be no shouting and running around, and you can put that football away right now for a start. Don't let me down, boys.' She straightened her shoulders and tucked a curl under the brim of her hat - a fedora I hadn't seen before, trimmed with a feather and perched at an angle on her fair hair. She has lovely hair, thick and wavy, which she usually wears caught up with combs at either side. 'Right, on we go. I'm gasping for a cup of tea after that mucky train.'

Stan and Alfie didn't say another word until we were safely in the kitchen with Gran, and even then they were ten times quieter than usual. I suppose it must have seemed very strange to them; the whole of our ground floor at home would have fitted into that one room. 'Where are the posh people?' Alfie whispered, and I had to explain that the Vyes were having their own tea in another part of the house where we couldn't even hear them. Mum helped Gran get ours ready and then Mr Huggins appeared with the huge silver teapot and hot water jug, followed by Alina with a tray of dirty cups and saucers. The boys sat and stared at them, speechless. They perked up when Sissy came through with the children, though: the chance of meeting Master Tristan was not to be missed.

'Can we go outside and play football?' Stan asked, and when Mum said yes, as long as they found a quiet spot well away from the house, Tristan went along as well. He looked scared to death of the big boys, but Stan let him carry the ball and I knew they'd make sure he was all right.

'Let's go for a walk,' Mum said quietly to me. 'We haven't had a proper talk in such a long while. Come on, I'll show you where your grandad and I used to work.' Mum had started off as a kitchenmaid but she became a groom alongside her father when most of the young men in the house went off to war.

Gran sent us off with her blessing, so we set off along the terrace towards the stable block. Mum glanced sideways at the windows. 'Are we allowed to walk here? It was out of bounds to us servants in my day.'

'Nobody's ever told me not to,' I said. 'Anyway, Lady Vye'll be in her room by now, and that's on the other side of the house so she won't see us.'

Isobel's Story

She took my arm. 'I didn't like to mention it in front of your gran but I'd say they've let the place go a bit, even since the last time I was here.'

Andreas was working in one of the flower borders so I stopped to say hello and introduce him to Mum. He shook her hand and they had a chat about roses; I think she liked him but it was hard to say for sure. 'He can draw beautifully,' I told her. 'He's painting a picture of Swallowcliffe for me as a leaving present.'

'That's nice of him,' she said. 'You've hardly been here long enough for leaving presents.'

By now we'd come to the stables. She reached up and ran her hand above the lintel. 'Da always used to keep the spare key up here. Yes! In we go.'

Here was another sad, ghostly place. Mum walked down one row of stalls and up the other, looking at a few of the name plates that were still on the wall. Mercury, Dolly and Snowflake; Daffodil, Moonlight, Bella and Cobweb. 'Did you know those horses?' I asked.

'In another life,' she replied. 'Most of them had gone by the time I was working as a groom. They were taken away to serve in the war, you know. None of them ever came back.' She rubbed her arms and shivered. 'Let's see how the harness room's looking.'

Now that was cosier; even the stag's head over the fireplace seemed to have a friendly gleam in its eye. A pink and yellow striped tie hung from one of its antlers which Mum unhooked and rolled into a ball, tutting. Walking round the small room, she ran a hand over a cracked leather saddle and jangled a row of chain straps with her fingers. 'Well, would you believe it?' She picked up a pair of dusty riding boots from the corner. 'These used to be mine, a hundred years ago. Fancy them still being here.'

'Don't you miss all this?' Maybe now was a good time to ask why Mum hardly ever came back to the Hall.

She sank into an armchair beside the fireplace while I sat on the table, swinging my legs. 'Not really. In a way, of course I do, but the things I miss disappeared so long ago it's hard to believe they ever existed. Working with Da and the horses - well, it all seems like a dream now.'

'Gran's still here, though, and the house. It probably hasn't changed that much.'

She wrinkled her nose. 'I'm not sure what to think about the house, to be honest. When there are five families sharing one outside toilet in the East End, it doesn't seem right that the Vyes should have this great big place all to themselves. The world's different now, and I can't say I'm sorry.'

'Not even a little bit? Gran told me about the fun you used to have in the servants' hall.'

'Oh, sometimes we were allowed to have a laugh, but we couldn't ever get above ourselves. Do as you're told and don't ask any questions, that's how

Isobel's Story

it used to be. And then the war came and suddenly everything changed. People realised the generals giving out orders and getting other people killed didn't always know best.' She chipped at a patch of dried mud on the floor with her shoe. 'Not that your gran would ever accept that.'

I knew what she meant but, all the same, it wasn't the whole story. 'But Gran loves this house, and the family, and she still does things her own way.' To be honest, I couldn't see that being a housekeeper was so very much worse than being a teacher. Everybody has to answer to someone, don't they?

'The Vyes look down on us, though - that's what I can't stand. Underneath, they think they're better than everyone else and they've no reason to. If you knew some of the things I do about that family, Is, you might feel differently about them.'

She wouldn't say any more, no matter how hard I pressed her, which seemed jolly unfair after dropping such a mysterious hint. Yet one of Mum's secrets was about to unravel all by itself, if only I'd known ...

Chapter Eleven

How shall we sing Thy song in a strange land?
How shall we not? For if my tongue should cleave
To the roof of my mouth and no song ever come
The dream must perish.
From *How Shall We Sing?* by Jewish writer and poet, Julian Drachman, 1939

WHEN THE BOYS AND I came down to breakfast the next morning, Mum was deep in conversation with Alina - or Angela, as we had to remember to call her.

'Listen to this, you lot,' she said. 'You might learn a thing or two.'

Besides the next day being Easter Sunday, apparently the festival of Passover had started. Mum knew something about it because she had a

Isobel's Story

Jewish boy in her class at school, she told us, and he'd written an essay on the subject.

'Passover comes from when Moses took the people of Israel out of Egypt,' Alina said. It was the longest sentence I'd heard her speak. 'And so quickly, they had no time to make good bread - only flat, like biscuits. So that is what we eat at Passover. It is called *matzah*.'

'Yes, and to get ready for Passover they have to clean the whole house so there isn't a crumb of ordinary bread left,' Mum added. 'Can you imagine, Ma? Clear the shelves, beat the rugs, sweep every inch of the floors.'

'Sounds like spring-cleaning to me,' Gran said, 'Funny them having the same custom as us.'

'A nice hygienic one, anyway,' Sissy put in, loading boiled eggs on to the children's breakfast tray. This was the strangest thing: instead of handing in her notice as Gran had predicted, Sissy had taken to Alina. Maybe it was because she worked so hard and had no intention of taking advantage. I'd seen them walking down to the village together with the girls when Alina had the afternoon off, and Sissy was the one Alina went to for help if she didn't know where something was. I felt a pang of jealousy that she had chosen Sissy for her friend rather than me but, then again, they were closer in age so it wasn't particularly surprising. They made an odd pair, though: large, placid Sissy next to slender, nervy Alina.

That afternoon, Mum and I went for a long walk through the woods and out into the fields beyond. The boys were building a den somewhere with Tristan and Gran was having a rest. 'She looks tired,' Mum said. 'I wish she'd call it a day, find a nice little cottage somewhere in the village and take things easy. It's not as though the Hall would crumble away without her - they could easily find another housekeeper.'

'Andreas's mother is desperate for a job in this country.' Before I knew it, I was telling Mum the whole story: what was happening to the Jews in Germany and all those other countries, Andreas coming over on the *Kindertransporte* and ending up in Mr Tarver's shop, how Gran had found Alina through the Jewish Refugee Movement. 'The trouble is, Lady Vye doesn't want any more foreigners in the house. That's why Alina has to be called Angela.'

Mum laughed. 'I wonder how long you'll be able to get away with that. Was it your idea? I'm surprised Gran agreed.' She looked out across the fields, shading her eyes against the sun. 'I'd forgotten how beautiful it was up here. Look at the colour of that grass! It's so fresh you can almost taste it.'

I tried to focus her attention. 'Is there anything Andreas's mother could do at your school, perhaps?'

'I'll ask, though I don't think so.' She squeezed my shoulder. 'Don't worry, Is. You needn't take every problem in the world on your shoulders.'

Isobel's Story

'But no one else seems to care!' I burst out. 'And when we go back to London, Andreas won't have anyone to speak up for him.'

She gave me a long look. 'Time was, you wouldn't have spoken up for yourself, let alone anyone else.'

Fat lot of good it had done, though; so far I'd got precisely nowhere and now we were going home. I'd let Andreas down. He'd soon forget about me and even if I did come back to Swallowcliffe in the summer, he and Alina were bound to be friendlier by then and wouldn't want me around. She couldn't go on resenting him being German for ever, and they had so much in common: so many shared experiences I couldn't understand. Just thinking about it made me feel grumpy and awkward. Suddenly I wanted to leave right there and then, without having to endure these last few pointless days, waiting to go.

We all went to church on Sunday morning - apart from Andreas, Alina and Gran, who stayed at home to start cooking the luncheon. Reverend Murdoch preached a sermon about standing shoulder to shoulder in God's army (we'd heard on the wireless that Italy had just invaded Albania - wherever that was - which might have had something to do with it) and we sang 'Onward Christian soldiers', but I found myself too unsettled by the way Mr Tarver was glaring at the Vyes to concentrate. Not just the Vyes, either. He kept shooting Mum and me spiteful looks, as though everyone from the Hall was part of a conspiracy to steal Andreas away. Thank goodness I'd managed to steer clear of the shop those past few weeks.

Gran set me to peeling potatoes as soon as we got back. 'And make sure you do plenty,' she said. 'There's two extra for luncheon today. The Hathaways are coming.'

She glanced at Mum across the table, and Mum blushed. Nobody noticed except me. I knew straight away that blush was significant; I'd never seen my mother look so uncomfortable. Mrs Hathaway's words suddenly sounded again in my head. 'Maybe there's still hope for them. You know my Philip never married again.' How could I have forgotten? Because what she was saying didn't make sense, I suppose. Dr Hathaway was one of the family: his mother was Lord Vye's aunt, so that made him Lord Vye's cousin. Surely there could never have been anything between him and my mother.

I kept an eye on Mum all the time we were preparing luncheon for the Vyes and ourselves. Because it was Easter Sunday there was a joint of meat for us in the kitchen, too, which we'd have after the Vyes had finished theirs. Mum didn't eat much and she was quiet all through the meal. Was she wondering where Dr Hathaway was, and maybe hoping to catch a glimpse of him? No, she looked more wary than anything else. After we'd eaten our

Isobel's Story

own dinner early, Stan and Alfie disappeared outside somewhere with Andreas and Tristan, but Mum and I were roped in to help with the washing up. We were halfway through when a fair-haired man in a brown tweed suit walked into the kitchen. 'I've come to see you're not wearing yourself out, Mrs S,' he said. 'That lunch was so delicious it had to be hard work.'

Mum turned around from the sink. Her face was flushed and damp from the heat of the water, her hair was falling out of its combs and she wore an old checked apron over her dress, but from the way he stared at her, she might have been a film star. Neither of them spoke for a few seconds and then he said, 'Grace? Nobody told me you were here.'

'Only for a little while.' Mum wiped her wet hands quickly down the apron. 'I've come to collect my daughter. We're going back to London tomorrow.' She pushed me forward. 'This is Isobel.'

'Hello.' He smiled at me distractedly, putting one hand on the back of a chair as if to steady himself. 'I'm Philip Hathaway. Dr Hathaway.'

There was an awkward pause. 'Dr Hathaway's been keeping an eye on me,' said Gran. 'But as we can see, I'm right as rain. Aren't I, Doctor?'

'Yes, no. Absolutely.' Now he was looking at Mum again. Her fingers dug into my shoulders as she held me in front of herself like a shield. 'Well, better get on, I suppose,' he said at last. 'Good to see you, Grace. And Isobel.' He went out of the room as though he were sleep-walking.

Mum didn't say a word but the next glass slipped out of her hands to shatter in the sink, and now I knew for certain there was a whole other story she hadn't told me. If only we weren't leaving the next day! Dr Hathaway still felt something for her, anyone could see that; it was as if an electric current had flowed through the air between them. I looked at Mum as though I'd never seen her before. She still had a lovely, open face, despite the fine lines on her forehead and crows' feet around her eyes, and even these few days in the country seemed to have taken years off her. Surely this was where she belonged, walking through fields in the fresh air, not grimy London streets piled high with sandbags.

But London was where we were heading and there was nothing I could do to change that, not now. When the kitchen was clean and tidy, I went up the back stairs and started packing my suitcase so it would be ready for the morning. Luckily it hadn't been too full in the first place, so the skirts and frock Gran had given me for my birthday fitted in without much trouble. When it was done, I kicked off my shoes and lay down on the bed, staring up at the ceiling and imagining myself back home. I must have fallen asleep because some time later a knock on the door woke me up and there was Andreas, holding a package in his hands.

Isobel's Story

'I have come to say goodbye,' he said, 'in case there is no time tomorrow. And to give you this.' He held the package out to me.

I rubbed my eyes, still half asleep, and invited him in. He took the flowery chair while I sat on the bed and tried to untie the string around the package. 'Here, I will help you,' he said, seeing me struggle, and came to sit on the bed beside me. Inside the brown paper was a framed painting of the view from the Fairview Tower, looking down on Swallowcliffe Hall. There was so much detail, it must have taken him ages.

I stared at the picture, not knowing what to say. 'Oh, Andreas! It's beautiful.'

'And there is me,' he said, pointing out a tiny figure standing in the rose garden. 'See? I am waving so when you look at this painting, you know I am saying hello.'

I smiled, though stupid, embarrassing tears were pricking at the back of my eyes. 'Thank you. I love it, truly I do. It's the most wonderful thing you could ever have given me.' Wrapping the picture up again in its brown paper, I packed it carefully away in my suitcase between the layers of clothes. Andreas patted the mattress beside him and I went to sit down again, trying not to feel awkward.

'You have been for me a good friend here,' he said. 'I wanted to say thank you for this.'

I stared down at my lap. 'There was so much

more I could have done! For your mother, and your cousin - '

'You did everything you can,' he said, 'and I know you try to help, that is important.' He took my hands and held them between his, and I truly thought my heart must have stopped beating. When at last I dared to look up, the sad, hungry yearning in his eyes made the breath catch in my throat. It was all there: the misery he must have kept bottled up for so long and which could never be properly expressed in words. There was no need to say anything. I knew how precious it was, this gift of trust. We moved closer -

And suddenly my bedroom flew door open. 'Isobel?' Mum was standing in the doorway, light flooding into the room from behind her. 'I thought I heard voices.'

Andreas sprang off the bed, his face scarlet. 'I come to say goodbye, that is all.'

She nodded and stepped aside, holding the door wide open. 'I assume you've said it now?'

He left without another word. Mum closed the door behind him with a sharp click. 'Well,' she said. 'It looks like we're leaving just in time. How could you be so stupid, Isobel? What on earth did you think you were doing, up here on your own with a boy?' She looked absolutely furious.

'It's not like you think. He doesn't have anyone else to talk to.' My voice trailed away. There was no

Isobel's Story

point trying to tell Mum how it was; she'd never understand.

She didn't. 'You're too young, and he's too ... too mixed-up. You must stay away from him from now on, do you hear? You should be thinking about School Cert and getting your life back on track, not messing around with boys.'

'We weren't messing around!' I protested. 'He needs someone to help him, Mum, honestly.'

'Maybe he does, but that someone doesn't have to be you.' She sat next to me on the bed. 'You're too gullible and you'll only end up getting hurt. Believe me, Is, I know. Wait till you're older and then find some nice boy from the same kind of background as you. It won't work otherwise.' She patted my knee and got up. 'You'd better stay up here this evening. I'll bring you a sandwich if you're hungry.'

That was almost a relief. I'd have been embarrassed to see Andreas again at supper in front of Mum. So I just lay on my bed for hours, listening to the everyday sounds of the house: the front door opening as Lord Vye took Wellington for an evening stroll around the gardens, Mr Huggins sounding the gong for dinner, busy footsteps as Alina tidied the bedrooms and turned down covers on the beds, Sissy running the twins' bath. There'd be time to say goodbye to the girls and Tristan tomorrow; just then I felt too sad. The room grew darker and eventually I heard Stan and Alfie coming up to bed. Mum put her head round the door but I pretended to be asleep and she went away. I couldn't sleep, though, not for ages. Apart from having had that nap in the afternoon, there was too much to think about. How could I leave Andreas like this? What if I never saw him again? How could we write to each other without Mum knowing? 'Find some boy from the same background as you. It won't work otherwise.' It suddenly struck me that she must have been thinking about Dr Hathaway.

At last I gave up on sleep and tried to read, although the words kept dancing in front of my eyes without making sense. Eventually, hours later, I fell into a doze and that strange dreamy state between sleeping and waking. I could hear a barn owl screeching somewhere in the woods, and smell the earthy, autumn scent of bonfires and burning leaves, but my eyelids were too heavy to force open. Yet I couldn't drift into deep sleep, either. A vague sense of unease nagged away at me, a feeling that something wasn't right. Was that Wellington barking? Could that unearthly sound really be an owl?

Suddenly I sat bolt upright in bed, terrified. The room was already thick with fumes as a silent, remorseless tide of soft grey smoke came seeping under our door.

Confusion. Panic. I couldn't see, couldn't breathe, couldn't think. Tearing off the blankets, I stumbled out of bed and across the room, my eyes

Isobel's Story

already smarting. It felt like walking through a pea-souper, except that I was floundering in a fog of smoke. 'Stan! Alfie!' I screamed, stumbling across their sleeping, sprawled bodies. 'Fire! Wake up!'

Seconds later they'd snapped into life, fumbling for clothes and belongings littered across the floor. 'No time. Go!' I heaved Alfie up by his pyjama jacket and pushed them both towards the door. But smoke was billowing underneath it by now and I didn't know what to do. Should we try and get out, or block the gap with a towel and open the window instead? Alfie made the decision for me, flinging the door wide open. As he vanished into the grey tunnel that used to be a corridor, I heard a dull roaring in the distance which frightened me even more. The thought of being trapped in this room was worse than anything and besides, I had to reach Mum and Gran. Following the boys outside, I tripped over something on the floor. My gas mask! It was there in its cardboard box next to my suitcase and Wellington boots, ready for the morning.

I usually hate this gas mask more than anything else in the world - that sickening rubbery smell, the feeling of claustrophobia when I put it on, 'Chin first!' as Mum's always reminding us - but just then I could have kissed the ugly thing. Even if it didn't keep out all the fumes, at least it meant I could open my eyes. It was even hotter with the mask on, almost suffocating, but I knew it'd be much harder to breathe without some help. Arms outstretched, I felt my way down the passage to Mum's room and bumped straight into her.

'Where are the boys?' she screamed, and I pointed past her down the corridor at the lumbering misty shapes that had to be my brothers. I hoped Alina was with them, too. Mum vanished for a second to reappear wearing her own gas mask, and then we both had to duck suddenly as a creature came swooping over our heads with a furious beating of wings, screaming like a banshee. Someone had let Punchy out of his cage. A shadowy figure emerged through the fog to meet us: it was Tristan. I herded him along the passage towards the clearer air at the other end and saw Stan reach out to take him.

Where was Gran? And Sissy and the girls? Their rooms must have been closer to the source of the fire because the heat blasted my chest as I went back to find them. Just as well I was still sleeping in a thick woollen dressing gown; it protected me from the flames that were surely close now. Gran was out of bed. I couldn't find her for a moment, then spotted her struggling to open the window. She resisted when I grabbed her arm, fighting against me. Perhaps she didn't know where she was, or perhaps she thought it would be safer to stay, but there wasn't a second to spare. If we didn't get out right away, the fire would cut us off. To my relief, Mum appeared behind me and together we took Gran under each

Isobel's Story

arm and hauled her out of the room.

Thank God! The door to the night nursery was opening and there stood Sissy with the girls. Except that she was only carrying one of them. It was Julia, and she was screaming, 'Nancy! Nancy!' over and over, and trying to wriggle out of Sissy's arms. Sissy was choking, but she managed to keep a tight hold on Julia and followed Mum and Gran down the passage with her. The smoke was so thick now I could hardly see, even with the mask, but I dropped to my knees and crawled the other way, towards the open door of the nursery. It was easier on all fours. Here were the flames: bright tongues beginning to lick around the margins of the room and creep up the curtains. There was no sign of Nancy anywhere and I couldn't bring myself to go any further. 'Nancy? Come out!' I screamed in despair from the doorway, knowing it was hopeless; she couldn't possibly hear me.

Suddenly someone pushed roughly past me and, by the time I looked up, a dark figure was plunging into the furnace. Another second and it had vanished, swallowed up in the billowing smoke. Who could possibly come out of that room alive? I began to back away, sobbing. And then I was hauled to my feet, and a limp bundle was shoved into my arms, and somehow I was running blindly down the passage and not alone any more because there was a retching, choking sound coming from somewhere behind me and a pressure at my back forcing me on. I looked down at the bundle in my arms. It was Nancy, lying very still. She didn't seem to be breathing.

Chapter Twelve

God is on high.
He can see you.
You will die. Men will die.
From *Reading Without Tears*, 1898

IT'S HARD TO REMEMBER exactly what happened after we ran down the corridor, and in what order. All I can come up with is a series of images: Lady Vye racing along the landing, silk nightgown streaming out behind her, to tear Nancy from my arms; Gran fighting for breath; Alina silently clutching a photograph of her family, wide-eyed; Julia shaking Nancy to wake her up with Sissy crying over them both; Punchy soaring up to settle at the very top of the house on the ledge beneath the cupola; Andreas holding out his arms, shreds of his pyjama sleeves falling away from the burnt skin underneath. He was the person who'd pushed past me to rescue Nancy.

Swallowcliffe Hall

What did we do next? Somebody brought blankets, I think, and Mr Huggins and Lord Vye carried Gran down the main stairs. We all went outside and before long, fire engines and an ambulance were tearing up the drive with their sirens blaring. Nancy and Andreas were loaded up, with only Lady Vye allowed to accompany her daughter. I could hardly bear to look at Andreas: a dressing had been put over his arms but his face was streaked black, his hair singed in places, and he was huddled over in pain. It was all I could do not to jump into the ambulance and throw my arms around him. And then I heard a commotion behind me: Mum was trying to persuade Gran to get in the ambulance too. 'No!' She tore herself out of Mum's grasp. 'I shan't go! You can't make me.'

'It's all right, Mrs S,' came a calm voice, and there was Dr Hathaway with his black bag. 'Sit down for a minute and I'll check you over myself.'

It was wonderful to feel that somebody was in charge who knew what they were doing. Gran let herself be led over to a bench and Mum knelt beside her. Even at a time like that, I couldn't help noticing how beautiful she looked, the ruddy glow of the fire on her face and her hair spilling over the blanket she'd thrown over her nightgown. 'Thank you,' she said to Dr Hathaway, which made me glad even though I was so upset and everything was so terrible.

'Shouldn't someone take a look at you, too?'

Isobel's Story

Mum asked me. 'You were in there longer than any of us.' But the gas mask had helped protect my face and lungs; apart from a sore chest and throat, and not being able to stop coughing, I felt more or less all right. So I stood on the grass with the boys and watched the Hall burn. The firemen had unravelled several endless hoses and Stan worked out they must have been pumping up water from the lake. Ash swirled on the air, timbers groaned and fell. Lord Vye paced up and down the terrace, shouting to point out where he thought new flames were gaining ground (although nobody seemed to be paying him a great deal of attention). So far the fire was contained in the old servants' quarters and the upper floors on our wing; if they could only keep it there, the damage to the main house might not be too bad.

Mr Oakes had come up from the gate lodge with his wife, still in her curlers. She offered to take the children with Alina and Sissy back there for what was left of the night, since the firemen wanted as many people as possible out of the way. They let me stay, thank goodness, to help look after Gran. I sat beside her on the bench while Dr Hathaway talked seriously to Mum a little way off where no one could hear them. He'd listened to Gran's chest with a stethoscope and given her some oxygen from a tank and mask the ambulance men had left behind. They'd obviously decided there was no point forcing Gran into hospital if she was so dead set against it.

Finally, miraculously, we heard someone say that the fire had been brought under control: there was no danger of it spreading to the rest of the house. Mum and I helped Gran back inside. There was a guest bedroom on the ground floor near the library where Lord Vye said she could go for the time being, which was decent of him, and a sitting room next door which we could use. Dr Hathaway brought the oxygen tank along and showed Mum how to use it, while I found sheets and blankets for the bed.

'Stop fussing! I'm all right,' Gran told us, but she clearly wasn't. She had to fight for every breath and I couldn't bear to hear the wheezing rattle in her chest. When we'd settled her into bed, Mum told me she'd doze in the chair beside for the bed for a while, just to make sure Gran was all right, so I could curl up on the sitting-room sofa. I made her promise to call me if Gran got any worse.

The next morning, it took me a good few seconds to work out where I was, before the acrid tang of smoke in my nostrils brought the nightmare flooding back. Yawning, I wrapped the blanket more tightly round myself and put my head around the bedroom door. Gran was alone in the room, looking very small in the high half tester bed. Her breathing seemed a little easier, though, so I set off in search of Mum. A couple of firemen talking together in the hall, brass helmets tucked under their arms, didn't

Isobel's Story

bat an eyelid as I walked past. They must have been used to seeing people in their night-clothes. All the windows in the house had been flung open and through one of them, I could see Lord Vye standing next to PC Dawes, the village bobby, and pointing something out to him on the roof. An air of unreality hung over everything.

The kitchen was more or less intact, amazingly enough, apart from a window being smashed and every one of Gran's precious pans black as coal instead of shiny copper, as well as the wall they were hanging on. Mum sat at the table, dressed in a man's shirt over a thick tweed skirt, having a cup of tea with Mrs Oakes. Grim Mrs Oakes had risen to the occasion. She had brought some clothes for me to wear, too: an old-fashioned liberty bodice, a pair of red flannel bloomers, a cotton blouse and a tartan kilt I could have wrapped twice round my waist. She was letting the boys sleep in, she said, and they could come up to the house when they were ready. 'They can stay with us in the gate lodge a while longer, Grace,' she added. 'And Isobel, too - I'm sure we can fit her in somewhere. You won't want to be going home until you see how your mother is.'

'What did Dr Hathaway say?' I asked Mum. 'Does he think Gran's going to be all right?'

She didn't answer straight away. 'He says she needs complete rest. I'm sure she'll be fine, but it might take a few days to be sure. And she might get worse before she gets better so we must be prepared for that.'

This wasn't the reply I'd been expecting, not at all. 'Lady Vye rang up from the hospital first thing,' Mum went on, changing the subject. 'Miss Nancy's doing very well. They don't think she'll have any lasting ill effects and she could even be home by the end of the week. That's wonderful, isn't it?'

Yes, it was. 'What about Andreas?' I asked. 'Has anyone heard how he is?'

'Oh, I'm sure he'll be fine.' She put the clothes in my arms. 'Now find somewhere to put these on and then come back here for some breakfast.'

'There's a lot of clearing up to be done,' Mrs Oakes added, 'and we might as well make a start. Many hands make light work.'

After getting dressed, though, I went outside for a look around first. The gaping windows of the old servants' quarters looked like sooty eyes, an ugly black smoke stain around each one, and the roof above was burnt completely through. The fire must have started there and leaped up the back stairs towards our bedrooms and the main roof of the house; a chimney stack had gone, although the attic dormer window further along was more or less intact. A few firemen and a couple of men from the village were still there, sorting through debris and gazing up at the roof from outside the house. And suddenly there was my suitcase! Sitting on the terrace

Isobel's Story

as though about to head off on holiday all by itself. It had changed colour from brown to black and the catches had fused with the heat, but Mr Oakes could probably force it open for me. It would be a relief to have my own clothes back but the only thing I really cared about was Andreas's painting. Dragging the case away, I left it against a wall to fetch later.

A little way off, Lord Vye was standing on his own with his back to the house, both hands deep in the pockets of his tweed jacket, gazing out across the lawn. I watched him from a distance, wondering what was going through his mind. Without making a conscious decision to move, somehow I found myself a few feet away, waiting for a chance to speak to him. We stood there for a minute or two and I was wondering whether to creep away unnoticed when he suddenly turned around.

'Yes? What is it?' His eyes were anxious and preoccupied. 'Ah. Lizzie, isn't it?'

'Isobel, sir,' I said.

'Isobel, of course. I was going to come and see you this morning - say thanks awfully for what you did, rescuing Nancy like that. Jolly brave of you, my dear. How are you feeling?'

'Not so bad, sir,' I said. 'But, really, it wasn't me who rescued Nancy, it was Andreas. He was the one who found her and brought her out of the nursery. I don't know how he had the courage, with the fire being so fierce, but somehow he managed it.'

'Did he really? Well, I must say, I'm extremely grateful to him. Awful thing.' He shook his head. 'You were lucky to get out alive. I must call in at the hospital and shake the boy by the hand, say thanks very much.'

Not the best thing to do, given Andreas's burns, but I didn't point that out. It was now or never; if I didn't speak up now, I'd probably never have another chance. 'There is something you could do for him, sir, that would mean more than anything. It's just that his mother is still in Germany, as you might know.'

'What? Oh yes, I think he did mention it.' Lord Vye had gone back to looking out across the park.

I decided to be blunt, having come this far. 'Well, I was wondering whether she might be a good person to help out here while my granny's getting back on her feet. Of course it's none of my business, really, but Andreas says his mother's a wonderful cook and I'm sure she'd work as hard as ever she could to get the house straight.'

'Get the house straight.' He gave a short laugh and glanced over his shoulder at the devastation behind us. 'It would take a miracle to do that. No, this is it, I'm afraid. The end of the road.' I didn't understand at first, but his meaning soon became clear. 'I've been putting off the inevitable for long enough. We shall have to lock the place up and walk away. As soon as the tenants have left the Dower House, we'll be moving in there.'

Isobel's Story

'But what will happen to Swallowcliffe?' I couldn't believe he was just giving up. He couldn't, not now! Not when the house needed us so badly.

'I did think the National Trust might step in, but this fire's put paid to that. The damage would cost too much to repair, and they weren't too keen on taking over the place in the first place.' He sighed. 'I'll tell you what will happen to it. The rest of the roof will cave in and eventually the ceilings will go. Then some tramp will camp out downstairs and burn what's left of the floorboards, while the garden turns to jungle and old motor cars start being dumped on the drive. When everything of any value has been stolen, rotted or burnt, the county council will declare what's left an eyesore and order the demolition boys in. And that will be that: hundreds of years of history gone for good.'

'But surely there's something we can do! Isn't there anyone who could buy the Hall?'

'Nobody wants the responsibility these days. No, I shall have to admit defeat.' He narrowed his eyes, still gazing out across the grass like a sailor scanning the horizon, and the next thing I knew, he was reciting poetry. '"The moving finger writes, and having writ, moves on; nor all your piety nor wit shall lure it back to cancel half a line, nor all your tears wash out a word of it." Do you know what that's about?' He didn't wait for an answer. 'Destiny, my dear. Events will take their course and there's nothing you or I can do to change them. Now, was there anything else you wanted?' The conversation was over.

I walked back to the house, thoroughly down in the dumps. There was no hope for the Hall now - let alone Andreas's mother - nor for Gran as its housekeeper. She wouldn't want to move to the Dower House any more than Lady Vye wouldn't want to have her there. Seeing Mrs Oakes in the kitchen, wearing Gran's apron, only underlined the fact that everything had changed. Still, somebody had to organise things indoors (Mr Huggins being occupied with matters outside) and Mrs Oakes seemed to be making a good job of it. She sent Alina off to tackle the hall floor, which was in a terrible state after so many firemen's boots tramping along it.

Stan and Alfie had appeared and were eating breakfast, dressed in another strange assortment of clothes. Alfie had been given a sailor's suit with a striped collar and shorts; he scowled ferociously at me so I wouldn't think of teasing him about it. After we'd had our porridge, she gave each of us buckets of soapy water and scrubbing brushes, and set us to work cleaning the kitchen walls. Scouring off the greasy, stubborn soot seemed to take for ever and we were still worn out after the night before, so it was hard going. Various people popped in and out: Dr Hathaway came to see how Gran was and so did

Isobel's Story

his mother, Reverend Murdoch appeared to tell us we were in his prayers, and then Eunice appeared out of the blue.

'I wouldn't desert you in your hour of need,' she said to Mrs Oakes. 'What a terrible thing to happen! I couldn't believe it. Mr Tarver's given me the day off so I could come and lend a hand.' It turned out that she'd been working in the shop since leaving the Hall, which must have been the perfect place for her: endless opportunity for gossip.

I was ready for a break by now and relieved when Mrs Oakes said I could go with Eunice and make up beds for the children and Sissy on the other side of the house so they'd have somewhere to sleep that night. 'I'll do the work,' Eunice said as soon as we were out of earshot. 'You look done in, which is hardly surprising after what you've been through. That Mrs Oakes is a slave driver.'

We had to take the marble stairs, of course, as the back staircase had been gutted in the fire; that was different and strange in itself. Collecting armfuls of sheets and blankets from the linen cupboard, we made our way along the corridor past the Vyes' suite (two connecting rooms with a bathroom in the middle), Lord Vye's dressing room and Lady Vye's sitting room. This part of the house was untouched, which seemed amazing after the horror of the night before. Had it really been no longer ago than that?

'We'd better put Sissy and Julia in the Red Room,'

Eunice said, opening the door. 'Mr Pennington was staying in here not so long ago so it won't be too damp. Now you sit in that chair and tell me all about it. You need to get everything off your chest.'

Although I didn't trust Eunice over much, she was a good listener and it *was* a relief to talk. I made sure she knew how brave Andreas had been, risking his life to save Nancy's.

'He probably didn't want to get into any more trouble,' she said, shaking out an undersheet which billowed like a puffy white cloud in the air before settling gently on the mattress.

'What do you mean by that?' I was genuinely puzzled.

'How do you think that fire started in the first place? It caught hold in Lord Vye's studio, that's what the firemen told PC Dawes, and who goes in there apart from His Lordship and the German boy? His bedroom's next door, isn't it? He probably dropped a cigarette or forgot to turn out the lamp. Those old oil lamps can be lethal if you leave them burning.' The electric lighting in the studio was dim, so Lord Vye had extra oil lamps dotted around for use at night.

I couldn't believe what she was insinuating. 'But Andreas doesn't smoke. And he's always really careful.'

She finished tucking under the sheet in a neat hospital corner. 'So who else was it, then? I know

Isobel's Story

you're soft on the lad but you've got to admit, it's a bit of a coincidence. He moves up to the Hall and hey presto, a few weeks later a fire starts right next to his room. Not that I'm saying he started it deliberately, mind. Though others might.'

'He might have died, Eunice!' I spluttered. 'Why would he do anything so dangerous? Besides, he could have run away and saved his own skin but he came back to help us.'

She gave me a cool look. 'It'd be in his interests to play the hero, wouldn't it? Anyway, he's still German even if he is Jewish into the bargain. He might be a spy for all we know. What if he wanted the lot of you to die in your beds and then had an attack of conscience at the last minute?'

I couldn't sit there listening to her a minute longer. 'That's rubbish, Eunice,' I said, getting up. 'You shouldn't go around saying such awful things. Now excuse me but I don't feel well. I'm going for a rest.'

'Think it over,' was her parting shot. 'Closing your eyes to the truth won't make it go away.'

I went downstairs to see how Gran was doing, trying to wipe Eunice's words out of my mind. I could just imagine her and Mr Tarver with their heads together behind the counter, concocting poisonous rumours and spreading them through the village. How could they? And then at the foot of the stairs, I suddenly stopped with one hand on the smooth mahogany banister, stock still. A liquid cascade of music came floating through the hall, the notes tumbling one after another and swelling into such a sad, sweet melody that my whole body tingled. I forgot all about Eunice, Mr Tarver and everything else in the world except that wonderful sound, sweeping over me like a wave and leaving such a sharp ache in my heart when it eventually faded away that I could have sat down and wept, there and then.

Trying to find out where it came from, I walked towards the drawing room and saw Alina sitting at the piano by the window, her mop and bucket propped forgotten against a chair. I'd never heard anyone else in the house ever use it. Eyes half shut, she rested her fingers gently on the keys and began to play again, coaxing out the notes as though the instrument was a living thing. I leaned against the door frame and gave myself up to the haunting sound; it soared out into our damaged world like a glimmer of hope, a promise that one day all would be well again. And then suddenly I noticed Lord Vye standing on the far side of the doorway into the dining room, just as rapt. He smiled and put his finger to his lips when he saw me start, and we stood listening silently together.

'What on earth are you doing?' A harsh voice rang out, shattering the silver stream of music into fragments. 'Who gave you permission to entertain

Isobel's Story

yourself in here?'

It was Lady Vye, back from the hospital. She pushed past me, strode across the room in seconds and slammed down the piano lid so abruptly Alina had to snatch her fingers away or they'd have been crushed.

'I'm sorry, madam.' She slid hastily off the piano stool. 'I thought nobody was here and my cleaning was finished. I forgot everything. I'm very sorry.'

'I should think so.' Lady Vye was pale and trembling with rage. 'This is a valuable instrument, not for the likes of you. How could you take advantage at a time like this?'

'It will never happen again, I promise,' Alina muttered, picking up her cleaning things and backing away.

Lady Vye watched her go. Alina was almost at the door when she called out, 'Just a minute, girl. "Angela", is it?' She pronounced the name with raised eyebrows. 'I think you and I need to have a little chat. Who taught you to play the piano like that, I wonder?'

Chapter Thirteen

Advice to Refugees

Refugees often give offence, mainly through ignorance, by taking positions out of their turn in queues at tram-stops, ticket offices and theatres. Take your place at the extreme end of the queue and wait your turn. The English love fair play.
From a leaflet given to refugee children arriving at Dovercourt camp in 1938/9

'IS EVERYTHING ALL RIGHT, Alina?' I'd been waiting for ages to find out, but the drawing-room door had remained stubbornly closed for so long I'd almost given up.

'I am not sure,' she said, leaning against the wall with her hands behind her back. 'Lady Vye was cross with me and now she knows I have come from

Isobel's Story

Poland. She says I cannot work here any more.'

'But that's awful!' I couldn't understand why she didn't look more upset. 'Where will you go?'

'There is a plan. When Lady Vye finished and went away, Lord Vye ask me about my family, what I am doing in this country, what instruments I like to play - all these things. Then he says he knows people in London and maybe I can stay with them. They love music and they are Jewish, too. He will speak to them on the telephone and ask. Today, even. It is kind of him when everything is still such a - ' she waved an arm round the hall, littered with buckets, mops and brooms, 'such a *balagan*.' I didn't know the word but it was easy to work out what she meant. A mess.

This was wonderful news: not only because Alina would be much better off with people like that, but because Lord Vye had taken an interest and done something to help her. Maybe the music had jolted him out of all that talk about moving fingers and destiny. 'It was lovely to hear you play,' I said, hoping she'd understand something of what it had meant to me.

'I have been wanting to, a long time. And why should I not when the piano is there and nobody uses it?' Alina's eyes flashed. 'She knows nothing of music, that stupid woman. I have decided to go anyway, before now, and she can make the bed herself. I do not come to this country to clean houses all day.' She untied her apron and bundled it into a ball, glaring at me.

'We couldn't think of anything else, that's all,' I stammered, taken aback by her blunt, angry words, 'and we hoped you'd stay.' We were trying to give you a chance, was what I wanted to add.

Her voice softened a little. 'I hope your grandmother is better soon. She was kind to me always.'

Yes, I was hoping the same thing. When I went to see how Gran was, later that morning, I caught a low hum of voices drifting out of the sitting room and found Mum talking to Dr Hathaway inside. The connecting door to the bedroom was closed and they both looked very serious - so serious that any excitement I might have felt at seeing them together vanished in a second.

'What is it?' I asked Mum as soon as Dr Hathaway had gone, saying he'd see himself out. 'Gran's not worse, is she?'

Mum sat down on the sofa. 'The doctor's been worried about her for a while, apparently. He says her lungs were in a bad way already and now this shock has knocked her for six. She ought to be in hospital but she's refusing point blank to go. What can we do? We can't drag her there, kicking and screaming. I shall have to write to your Aunt Hannah and see what she thinks.' She buried her face in her hands. 'Oh, how can I have let it come to this? Why didn't I

Isobel's Story

keep more of an eye on her?'

I sat next to her, rubbing her back. 'It's not your fault. You know what Gran's like, she won't listen to anyone. She'd sooner wear out than rust out, that's what she told me.'

Mum pushed back her hair, smiling ruefully. 'I'm so glad you've had this time together. She's loved having you here, I can tell.'

'And I've loved it too. But, Mum, Lord Vye says the family's going to move out of the Hall. What's going to happen to Gran? Where will she live when she's better?'

'Let's take it one step at a time.' A cold hand gripped my heart and squeezed it tight. Did that mean she thought Gran wasn't going to recover? She sighed, leaning back against the sofa cushions. 'I should have come down here more often.'

'Why didn't you?' Now seemed as good a time as any to ask, now we were alone together in this quiet, cosy room and Mum was obviously in a mood to talk. With the curtains half drawn against the outside world and only a soft golden light from the lamp in the corner, it felt almost like being in church.

'I don't know,' she said. 'This place draws you in, somehow. Maybe I was frightened that I wouldn't get away again, that I'd end up chained to the stove for ever. I've made a life for myself on my own terms but it's not the life your granny wanted for me.' She reached out for my hand. 'Oh, Izzie, what a mess

I've made of everything! Let's promise always to talk to each other, shall we? I can't bear to think of you making the same mistakes I have.'

I took a huge risk. 'Is that why you don't want me to see Andreas? Because of you and Dr Hathaway?'

That made her drop my hand pretty quick. 'There is no "me and Dr Hathaway". Have you been listening to gossip? All that business was over and done with years ago.' She got up abruptly. 'I'm going to check on Gran. Can you see what the boys are up to?'

So much for always talking to each other. And it wasn't over and done with as far as Dr Hathaway was concerned, I could have told her that.

We had baked potatoes for dinner, with some cheese from the larder and two loaves of bread Eunice had brought up from the shop (which was thoughtful of her, I suppose). It was a funny sort of meal. Mr Huggins forgot to say grace and didn't stay long; he was sorting through some old trunks upstairs which had been saved from the attic storerooms. Julia was refusing to eat until Nancy came home and nothing Sissy said could make any difference, while even Tristan and my brothers had lost their appetite. It was noticeable that Eunice sat as far away from Alina as she possibly could - not that Alina seemed to care. In fact she was slightly more cheerful than usual, if anything. I suppose the thought of better prospects was cheering her up. The rest of us were exhausted, though, and we each had plenty to worry about.

After dinner, Sissy took all the children back to the gate lodge for a rest and I told Mum she should have a sleep too - I'd sit with Gran for a while. She was dozing when I took the armchair next to the bed. This new grandmother took some getting used to, lying there so still and helpless with her hair in a long plait over the pillow instead of its usual neat bun. I felt just as guilty as Mum, looking at her. Why hadn't *I* noticed she wasn't well? Please get better, Gran, I prayed silently, and we'll do all sorts of nice things together - the three of us. I hooked my legs over the arm of the chair and rested my head against a cushion, letting my thoughts run away with themselves. The awful thing was, now Eunice had got me wondering how the fire *had* actually started. What if Andreas had been careless after all? The possibility that anyone could have set fire to the Hall deliberately - least of all him - was too awful to contemplate. I closed my eyes and tried to clear my mind.

I woke to find Gran propped up on the pillows, smiling at me. 'I reckon you should be the one in bed,' she said. 'Shall we swap places?'

'How are you feeling?' I shook my head to clear it and focused on her face. 'Would you like a glass of water?'

'No, thank you, lovie.' She lay back and closed her eyes. 'I seem to be rather tired, that's all.'

I smoothed the sheet, trying to make her as comfortable as possible. A few seconds later, her eyes snapped open and she gripped my hand. 'Don't let them put me in hospital, will you? Once they take you off to one of those places, you never get out. I want to die in my own bed.'

'Gran! Don't talk about dying.'

'Why not? It comes to all of us sooner or later, and I'm quite ready to go.' She might have been talking about a shopping trip. 'So long as I can stay here at Swallowcliffe, that's all I ask.'

I couldn't let her be so passive, so accepting. 'But if you went into hospital, they'd be able to make you better. Then you could come out and rest and I'd look after you, just like you looked after me when I was poorly.' The very thought of it made me ashamed.

'You're a good girl, Izzie. I wouldn't have missed our time together for anything.'

'Well, it's not over yet,' I said desperately. 'Now don't wear yourself out. Go back to sleep and you'll feel better when you wake up.'

'No, I want to talk. I want you to understand.' She squeezed my hand, then let it go. 'I've had a happy life, all in all - so many wonderful memories to look back on. But I miss your grand-dad, and my darling boy, Tom. Lately I've been feeling them very

Isobel's Story

close by. If I went off to join them, would it be such a bad thing?'

'Don't talk like that, Gran! I can't bear it.' I lowered my head so she couldn't see the tears welling up in my eyes. 'It would be a bad thing for me, a terrible thing.' I couldn't say any more.

'Oh, you'll be all right. You'll be sad, of course, but you've got your mother to look after you and the rest of your life to be getting on with.' She coughed. 'Maybe I will have that drink of water after all.'

I went to pour a glass from the jug on the side table, trying to control my feelings but within a whisker of throwing myself on the bed and crying like a baby.

She took a sip. 'Of course it's wrong to have favourites, and don't ever breathe a word of this to your aunties, but I've always had a soft spot for Grace. Such a fierce little thing, she was! So proud. I tried to protect her, but it didn't do any good. She had to have her own way.'

Just like you, I thought, though I knew better than to say so.

Gran lay back on the pillow. I'd just decided she'd gone back to sleep when she suddenly said, 'There is something you could do for me, dear. You know that pretty writing desk in the far corner of the library?' I nodded. 'Well, if you take the top righthand drawer out, there's a little compartment behind it. There are some letters in there. If anything should happen to me, will you give them to your mother? She'll understand.'

'What shall I tell her?' I asked, but Gran didn't answer. She was soon properly asleep while I sat in the chair, watching her. I wanted to stay close by for ever, but a little while later Mum came in and told me she would take over, in a voice that couldn't be argued with.

'You can go down to the gate lodge for a rest as well,' she said. I didn't want to - not when my head was buzzing with so many thoughts and unanswered questions that going to sleep would be out of the question - but she stood at the door and watched me go; I didn't even have a chance to call by the library and look for the mysterious letters. There was no hurry to find them, though. Nothing was going to happen to Gran if I could help it.

It felt good, walking down the drive in the fresh, faintly smoky air, away from the chaos and muddle of the house. I'd managed to force the suitcase open and change into my own clothes which was an important step towards feeling more normal. Pushing my hands deep into the pockets of my coat, I stood looking at the front door of the gate lodge and wondering what to do. Taking a rest seemed feeble, unadventurous; I wasn't an invalid any more, and there was a shilling buried amongst the crumbs and fluff in my lefthand coat pocket. I turned my back on the lodge and headed away from

Isobel's Story

Swallowcliffe towards the bus shelter. Gran wasn't the only person on my mind. An image kept flashing into my head of Andreas, alone in hospital with no one to visit him, no one who really cared how he was - and his mother, hundreds of miles away, not even knowing what had happened to him.

It took nearly an hour for the bus to arrive, another half hour as it pottered along the narrow country lanes before eventually arriving in Hardingbridge, and twenty minutes on top of that for me to walk from the bus stop to the hospital. 'Visiting time's nearly over,' said the stern-faced lady behind a desk in the hall. 'You'll have to hurry. Which ward do you want?'

'I'm not sure. The men's ward?' Maybe they wouldn't even let me go there on my own. 'I've come to see my ... cousin,' I added. 'He's about sixteen or seventeen.'

'Don't you know which?' She looked at me over her glasses. 'Try Carnegie first, the children's ward: end of the corridor, turn right, right again and up the stairs. If he's not there he'll be in the men's. Faraday, it is: straight on, left at the end of the corridor, first right and second on the left.'

Andreas wasn't in Carnegie, which took me a good five minutes to find. By the time I'd made my way to Faraday, I was so flustered and so worried visiting hours might have ended for the day that I simply marched straight in. Several elderly men were asleep, sunken mouths open and teeth in a glass on the bedside table; a few had visitors sitting quietly on iron-framed chairs next to the bed. A large man wearing a neck brace was surrounded by his family - wife seated, children standing in a line from tallest to shortest - whose heads immediately swivelled around to stare at me as I walked down the room. I didn't care. Andreas was sitting in bed in a far corner of the ward, wearing a faded pyjama top with both sleeves cut away. His left arm and hand were completely covered in bandages while his right arm was strapped down to the wrist, and the skin on one side of his face was red and tight, glistening with some kind of ointment. It was painful even to look at.

He stared at me too, as if he couldn't believe his eyes. 'Isobel! What are you doing here?'

'Thought you might want a visitor.' I took the chair, trying not to notice how loud our voices sounded in the sepulchral hush. 'Sorry I haven't brought you anything. It was a spur of the moment decision.'

'That's all right. It is good to see you. Please, tell me how is everybody?'

I leaned forward. 'Nancy's going to be fine. Isn't it wonderful? You saved her life and I told Lord Vye so. Has he been in to see you? He said he would.'

'Thank you. I worried about her.' He shifted in the bed, and I could tell the effort hurt. 'No, Lord

Isobel's Story

Vye has not been here. He is busy, I think. What happens with the house?'

'Well, you haven't got a bedroom any more and the studio's gone. That wing's pretty much gutted but the main house isn't too badly damaged. It's mostly the back staircase and the night nursery that were affected. The firemen think a window at the top of the stairs must have been open and the air coming in sucked the fire up there.' So Eunice had told us over dinner; trust her to have found everything out. 'But how are you feeling?' I tried not to look too obviously at his bandages.

'Not so bad. They will keep me here for a week or maybe longer. I am sorry for my face. Does it look bad?'

'No, not at all! Just a bit red.' I wanted to hug him. 'You were so brave, bringing Nancy out of the nursery. How did you find the courage?'

'There was no time to think, and I knew she would be under the bed. That was my place to hide when I thought the Nazis will come.' He smiled at me lopsidedly. 'You were brave, too. What happens to the girl who was afraid of everything?'

'But I couldn't go in there. If it had been up to me - ' A scraping of chairs on the linoleum floor made me look around; people were gathering up their bags and saying their goodbyes. A clock on the wall read five to four, and visiting hours were obviously coming to an end. There was something I had to ask.

Swallowcliffe Hall

'Andreas, can you tell me what you remember about the fire? From the beginning, when it started.'

'I was deep asleep,' he said. 'When I wake up, the studio already burns very badly and I cannot go through. I run outside and see the fire up the side of the house, but there is no way in - the front door is locked. I have to break a window in the kitchen and climb by that. The back stairs are on fire, so I run up the main stairs and along the passage to find you. And the rest you know.' He looked at me curiously. 'Why do you ask this question?'

I tried to keep my voice light. 'Oh, no reason in particular. Only trying to get the picture straight.'

He must have read something in my face. 'No, that is not all. A policeman came here this morning and ask me these same things.' His voice grew louder, too loud for the quiet room. 'You think this fire is because of me, don't you? It is something I have done!'

One of the nurses looked over at us, then glanced pointedly at the clock. It was two minutes to four and I was the only visitor left. 'No, that's not what I think at all,' I assured him, getting up. 'Of course it was an accident, I know that. But you see, apparently the fire started in the studio and nobody else apart from you ever uses it except Lord Vye, and he wouldn't be there in the middle of the night, would he? Maybe if you'd left one of the lamps burning or something…'

Isobel's Story

'I never do this!' Andreas pushed himself bolt upright with his better arm, glaring at me. 'Always I am careful.'

'I know, that's why I wanted to ask you,' I gabbled. The nurse was walking towards us, her shoes squeaking over the linoleum floor. 'Try to think, Andreas! Can you remember anything else that might explain it?'

'Time for you to be going, young lady.' I felt a hand under my elbow that meant business.

'Just one minute, please, dear Nurse Phillips.' Andreas gave his crooked smile and I could see her melting. 'I must say this very important thing to my friend, Isobel.'

She folded her arms. 'You can have one second. And it better *had* be important.'

I bent down beside the bed. 'For some time, I think someone comes near the studio at night,' he said urgently. 'I hear a noise in the garden - two, maybe three times. And this night, I see from outside that a window of the studio is open when always I close them. What if somebody else comes in and starts the fire?'

'But why would anyone do that? It doesn't make sense.'

He grabbed my arm with his free hand. 'It is all I can think. Please, Isobel! You must help. They must not think this bad thing is because of me. If they send me back to Germany then it is the end of everything. There is nothing I can do here in this hospital. Can you find out what happens? Promise me you will!'

Chapter Fourteen

Advice to Refugees

Do not criticise England or the English. Do not explain, however truthfully, that certain things are much better managed in Germany. The English are quite capable and quite ready to do their own criticism of their Government and institutions.

From a leaflet given to refugee children arriving at Dovercourt camp in 1938/9

ALL THE WAY BACK on the bus, I thought about what Andreas had asked. How could I possibly find out whether someone had broken into the studio and started a fire, accidentally or otherwise? It crossed my mind that maybe this idea of the open window and an intruder was a story he'd come up with to distract attention away from himself. No, I knew him better than that. If he'd had anything to do with the fire, he'd have said so, I was sure of it. Even if it meant he might have been thrown out of the house, though? Possibly sent back to Germany? I sat there with the sunlight warm on my face, and wondered.

When I arrived at the Hall, Mum was in her usual place, the chair next to Gran's bed. Tendrils of hair stuck out all around her face and she looked harried. 'What's the matter?' I asked. 'Is everything all right?'

Gran was shifting about uncomfortably and her face seemed subtly different; she was pale, but patches of colour burned in each cheek. There was a bowl of water and a face cloth on the table beside her and a smell of *eau de cologne* in the air.

'She's running a temperature,' Mum said. 'Dr Hathaway called in this afternoon and he says she must have developed an infection. I'm glad you're here, Izzie. What are the boys up to? Are they all right?'

Luckily I'd called in at the gate lodge and seen Stan, Alfie and Tristan absorbed in an elaborate game with an army of lead soldiers which Mr Oakes had brought down from the house. The firemen had rescued a wooden toy chest from the schoolroom, as well as the rocking horse and the dolls' house. Miss Murdoch's charts and mottoes on the wall were black with smoke, but who cared about those? 'The boys are fine,' I told Mum. 'Busy down at the lodge with Tristan.'

She let out a sigh of relief. 'That's one thing less to worry about. Lady Vye came in earlier as well, to see how your granny was doing. She's come up with a plan. Mrs Oakes is going to take over as housekeeper for the time being, so she and Mr Oakes will be moving up to the house. It makes more sense for them to be here, keeping an eye on everything, and we can look after Gran in the gate lodge. The only trouble is, Dr Hathaway says she's too ill to go anywhere for the moment. We'll have to wait till her fever's broken.'

'How long will that be?'

'I don't know. Maybe a day or so.' She handed me the bowl. 'Could you get some more cold water, lovie? This is tepid already.'

When I came back, Gran was tossing and turning on the pillow. 'Don't burn the sausages,' she muttered. 'And there mustn't be any white stripes either. Nice and golden all over.'

'She's been saying all sorts of strange things,' Mum said, smiling in spite of herself as she wrung out the face cloth. 'Just now it was something about breaking the china and getting her cards from Lady Vye.'

'It's nice of Lady Vye to let us stay in the gate lodge for a while, isn't it? Where you used to live.'

That seemed surprisingly thoughtful of her.

Mum leant forward and gently sponged Gran's face. 'I suppose so,' she muttered. 'But all this bowing and scraping and having to be grateful to the Vyes - I can't bear it. I wish they didn't have to be involved.'

'What's going to happen in the long run?' I asked. 'To us, I mean. There's only another week or so left of the school holidays.'

'We'll have to see how Granny is. Maybe by then she'll be well enough to come back to London for a while.'

I couldn't imagine Gran in London for more than a few days; it wasn't her kind of place. Whenever she came to see us, she and Mum usually ended up tight-lipped by the end of the visit, and I knew they were both relieved when it was over. And what about Mum's job? How could she work and look after an invalid at the same time? I took a deep breath. 'I think Gran would sooner stay where she is.'

'She may not have much choice. I can't look after her here. What else are we going to do?' Mum tipped the flannel back into the bowl, stifling a yawn. She didn't protest when I offered to take over so she could go off for a rest or a cup of tea.

Time passed very slowly. It felt as though the whole world had shrunk to the size of this one room and nothing mattered beyond it. I dozed in the chair for a while, on and off, but couldn't let myself fall deeply asleep. Gran was restless and when I wiped

Isobel's Story

her face, the cloth grew warm between my fingers. I couldn't believe she'd gone downhill so quickly. The worst of it was, she seemed so agitated and uncomfortable. 'I did what I thought was best,' she said at one point. 'You can't blame me for that.'

'It's all right, Gran.' I smoothed the hair off her burning forehead. 'No one's blaming you for anything.'

'You told me to do it, Iris,' she said, looking straight at me. 'I only took the baby because you asked me to. And I found a good home for him, truly I did!'

What was that? She must have thought I was her old friend, Iris Baker. So Iris had had a baby, and Gran had taken him away somewhere? There was probably one reason for that: Iris couldn't have been married. She must have been one of the fallen women Reverend Murdoch collected for. I stared at Gran, wondering if any of this could be true or if it was all a product of the fever. 'Here, have a drink,' I said, holding the glass to her lips. Half of me wanted her to stop this incoherent rambling; the other half was eager to find out more.

Gran pushed the glass away. 'Mrs Chadwick knows all about you, Iris, and I gave her the locket for Ralph when he's older. She's a kind woman, she'll care for him like one of her own. He's at a vicarage. That's nice, isn't it?'

'Yes, it's lovely,' I said, since she seemed to

want an answer.

She sank back on the pillow. 'May I have some elderflower cordial? Nobody makes it like you.'

'Here we are.' I offered her the glass again and this time she took a sip, though it made her cough. She turned her head to one side, closed her eyes and didn't say anything else.

It was strange: the name Chadwick sounded familiar to me. Ralph, too. Ralph Chadwick - now where had I heard that name before? Suddenly I sat bolt upright in the chair, the skin on both arms tingling as though an electric current had passed through them. There had been a Mr Chadwick here, in this very house! I'd shown him around with his wife, the day we heard Hitler had invaded Czechoslovakia. What had she called him? Something beginning with R, I was sure of it. And he was the right kind of age to be Iris's son - about ten years older than Mum.

No, it was too much of a coincidence; there were bound to be a number of R. Chadwicks in the world. I racked my brains to come up with some more details about the man I'd met. He'd been in the army and stayed at the Hall when it was a convalescent home, that was it. Had Gran seen him again then? There must have been so many patients passing through, she might not have known all their names. He'd just retired from teaching, his wife had said. She'd also said - and now a tingle danced the length of my spine - that his father had been the

Isobel's Story

vicar of a nearby village.

'He's at a vicarage. That's nice, isn't it?'

So Iris's son had come back to the house where his mother used to work. He didn't know anything about her or the Swallowcliffe connection, it was obvious, and Gran had had no idea he was there. We had to bring them together!

'What are you looking so excited about?' Mum was back, carrying a basin, a clean face cloth and a towel on a tray.

'Gran's been talking about the old days. Do you know she had this friend called Iris Baker? We visited her grave when I first came down here.'

'Yes, I've heard about Iris.' Mum put the tray down on a side table. 'What exactly did Gran say?'

I hesitated, suddenly shy about raising such a sensitive matter. 'Well, apparently Iris had a baby and Gran took him away to a vicarage to have him adopted.'

'I knew Iris had had a baby,' Mum said, after a pause, 'but I thought it had died along with her in the workhouse. She wasn't married, you see, so she lost her job at the Hall and ended up there. The Vyes threw her out to fend for herself.'

'Yes but, Mum - the amazing thing is, he was here!'

'What do you mean?' she asked sharply, her face darkening. 'Who was where?'

'Iris's son!' My voice was high with the thrill of

it all. 'Ralph Chadwick, his name is, and I showed him around the Hall a couple of months ago. He'd stayed here in the war when the house was a convalescent home. It's the same person, I know it is! We have to tell Gran as soon as she's better.'

'No.' Mum covered the distance between us in a few paces. 'You're not to breathe a word to her about any of this. Do you understand?' She took me by the shoulders. 'Not a single word. It would be too much of a shock.'

'He was so nice, though,' I protested. 'Well-dressed and pots of money. Wouldn't Gran want to know he'd turned out all right? She loved Iris, didn't she? And she sounded so worried just now when she was talking about it.'

'There are things you don't know about the whole sorry business. Let sleeping dogs lie, Isobel, that's the best thing. Now off you go. There are sandwiches in the kitchen for supper.'

She was treating me like a child again, and I hated it. If there were things I didn't know, why couldn't she explain what they were? What possible harm could there be in telling Gran her friend's baby was now a respectable grown-up man? And not only Gran - there was Ralph Chadwick to think about, too. Didn't he have the right to find out who his mother was, and talk to someone who had known her? I had discovered something important but Mum was trying to sweep it under the carpet. Well,

Isobel's Story

I wouldn't let her.

It would be the second night I'd spent under a blanket on the sitting-room sofa, which wasn't quite long enough so I had to lie on one side with my knees drawn up. Dr Hathaway came to check on Gran again at about ten and have another of those serious conversations with Mum. Even with my ear to the door, all I could catch was the odd phrase: 'complete rest', 'pneumonia', 'time will tell'. Still, at least they were spending some time together. I liked Dr Hathaway. He was obviously fond of Gran and, as for Mum - he couldn't take his eyes off her. It was as though he couldn't quite believe she was actually there.

I'd just changed into my nightgown when an uncomfortable thought struck me: maybe I should go and find those letters Gran had mentioned. It meant admitting to myself how ill she was, but on the other hand, there might not be a better chance to retrieve them; nobody would be anywhere near the library at this time of night. I sat on the edge of the sofa, wondering what to do, before at last letting myself quietly out of the room. I could always put the letters back in the morning.

Moonlight streamed in through the library windows so there was no need to switch on a light. Dark outlines of furniture were dotted about like islands in the sea: comfortable chairs for reading, side tables with lamps, a globe on its stand, two huge urns, one on either side of the marble fireplace. It was strange how this fire had opened up the house, I thought, making my way over to the writing desk; it felt as though we had the right to go wherever we pleased. Everyone used the same staircase now, and there was Gran in one of the guest bedrooms with Sissy and the girls upstairs, right next door to the Vyes. No wonder Lady Vye was off to London.

The desk was a lovely thing, standing on thin, elegant legs with painted oval panels and swags on its many drawers. I sat down on the spindly chair beside it and carefully eased out the top right drawer, holding my breath. Surely this space was too small to hold anything? I felt all over the smooth wooden cave the drawer had left behind. Nothing. Maybe someone had found the letters first, or maybe Gran had made a mistake. Had she put them there, or merely been told about them? I sat back on the chair, looking at the desk. There was another possible drawer but it was under one of the painted ovals at the extreme righthand side - not exactly on top. Still, it was worth a try.

This drawer fitted more snugly and I had to tug hard on the brass handle before it finally came all the way out. The drawer was shorter than it should have been, I could tell, and the back of the desk behind it seemed foreshortened too. I had to risk turning on the lamp. Yes! There was a tiny ring set into the wooden panel. I pulled it and the

Isobel's Story

whole piece came away in my hand. Reaching in, my fingers touched paper. There were three letters jammed into that small space, all of them addressed to Philip Hathaway Esquire at Swallowcliffe Hall in handwriting I recognised as my mother's. And the strange thing was, none of them had been opened.

I sat looking at those letters for some time. The ink had hardly faded, even though they'd been written over twenty years before: they were postmarked Glamorgan, October 1916. I knew Mum had worked as a land girl in Wales for part of the war. She must have written to Dr Hathaway from there but he'd never got the letters. Somebody - Gran, I supposed - had intercepted and hidden them. It would have been easy to do with the butler's help, since all the post went through him. So that was why Mum was so sniffy with Dr Hathaway. She *was* proud, and to have written to him not once or twice but three times without any reply would have been more than she could bear.

And why had Gran done it? I knew the answer to that question. She was trying to protect Mum because Dr Hathaway came from a different class and she thought it would never work. Mum had been hurt anyway, though, and as far as I could see, Dr Hathaway still loved her. Perhaps Gran realised that too, which was why she'd asked me to make amends by giving Mum her letters back. I turned out the lamp and tucked them in my dressing-gown pocket. There was so much to think about, and I had to be sure of doing the right thing.

Chapter Fifteen

Advice to Refugees

Take particular care not to push yourself forward in shops. There are ample supplies of food and clothing in the country. Take your turn, ask for no more than your due ration, and the English shopkeeper will treat you fairly and courteously. Do not try to barter about prices. The English shopkeeper has fixed prices ...and it gives offence to imply that they are too high.

From a leaflet given to refugee children arriving at Dovercourt camp in 1938/9

I WAS WOKEN BY SUNSHINE leaking round the edge of the heavy velvet curtains. Mum hadn't called me; I'd slept right through the night until the kind of morning where anything seems possible, and Gran was lying peacefully in her bed next door.

'The fever's broken,' Mum said, throwing herself into an armchair. 'I think she's going to be all right. Oh, Izzie! I can't tell you the relief. Maybe later on today we'll be able to move down to the gate house so I can keep a proper eye on the boys, too. Mrs Oakes and Sissy can't look after them for ever.'

'I'll go and sit with Gran.' I stretched my stiff legs and then swung them on to the floor. 'You must be worn out.'

'No, it's all right. I think we can leave her alone for a while now. Tell you what, though.' She reached for her handbag. 'After breakfast, why don't you walk down to the shop and buy a quarter pound of those barley sugars she likes? The fresh air will do you good. And a bottle of elderflower cordial, if they have it. She was asking for some a little while ago.'

I hadn't been to the shop for ages, but somehow the thought of seeing Mr Tarver wasn't so frightening now - not after what we'd been through, and Andreas out of the way in hospital. What could Mr Tarver say to hurt either of us? After taking a quick look at my granny, I got dressed slowly and went off to wash in the cloakroom. We'd been camping out for long enough; it would be good to sleep in a bed again. Through the open drawing-room door, I could see Mr Huggins and Mrs Oakes hoisting a dustsheet over the bureau bookcase. They were putting the house to bed, Mum had told me.

Isobel's Story

Some favourite pieces of furniture were going down to the Dower House but the rest would stay under covers until Her Ladyship decided what was to be done with it.

'How is Mrs S?' Mr Huggins called to me as I went past.

'Much better, thank you. I'm going down to the shop to fetch her some things, but I'll come back and help you after. Are the boys causing you any trouble?' I asked Mrs Oakes as an afterthought.

'Mr Oakes has them washing the motor,' she replied. 'The devil makes work for idle hands and there's plenty to be done. That Alina's gone, left early this morning.'

'Without saying goodbye?' I was disappointed, but not exactly surprised.

'She gave Sissy her forwarding address in case any letters arrive.' Mrs Oakes gave the dustsheet a vigorous tweak. 'Well, she'll probably be happier in London. She was a good worker, though - pity to lose her when we need the help.'

We were all about to go our separate ways. I shouldn't have liked to be Mr and Mrs Oakes, left alone to hold the fort in a couple of rooms. Swallowcliffe was soon going to look like Sleeping Beauty's castle inside as well as out, I thought, walking past a row of white-shrouded chairs in the hall. They would stand there, lonely and unloved, while moths chewed through the calico covers and the silk upholstery rotted away underneath.

After eating a slice of bread and butter standing up in the kitchen, I went out through the blue door, its paint now blistered and peeling. The smoke-blackened servants' wing made me instantly think of Andreas. Even if it would be impossible to find out how the fire had started, at least I could see if anything of his was salvageable from the ruins. It hit me for the first time as I stood in the shell that had once been his bedroom, that of course all his precious photographs and letters had gone. The only furniture still standing in the room was an iron bedstead; everything else had been burnt to a cinder. I turned over a heap of charcoal and ash with my foot, searching for fragments. There was nothing left - only, after ten minutes' or more diligent searching, a piece of sooty metal that had once been a silver spoon with the initial 'R' on its handle. It seemed very hard that someone with so little in the first place should have to lose even those few things he had.

His Lordship's studio was completely gutted. The paintings would have gone up in a second, but the big table on which the servants used to take their meals had been burnt, too, and it had always looked so solid and indestructible. I remembered taking Andreas's picture to show Lord Vye and Mr Pennington after the disastrous dinner party. What a long time ago it seemed! The windows were all open now, and the glass in them either shattered or

Isobel's Story

melted into rivulets like frozen teardrops down the wall. Why would anyone have wanted to break into the studio? There was nothing of any value here.

Crouching down, I poked about in a layer of debris directly under the windows with Andreas's spoon in the faint hope there might be something of interest. After a few minutes, it snagged on something: a broken chain, with a hollow cylinder attached to one end. I held the thing up to the light, wondering what it could be. The cylinder had a curved mouthpiece and a rectangular slot cut into it, like a miniature post box. It was a whistle. When I rubbed away the smuts on my skirt, three initials above the slot were revealed. ARP, I read, and everything became suddenly clear.

My feet carried me down to the village shop without my head having much to do with it. I could see it all: Mr Tarver snooping around outside the studio at night under the pretext of carrying out his duties, hoping to find something incriminating. He just couldn't bear the fact that Andreas had escaped his clutches. Perhaps he was the one spreading the spying rumours and thought he might find something to back them up. He must have struggled through the window somehow, losing his ARP whistle in the process, and lit a lamp rather than turn on the main light which would be easily seen. Maybe he thought someone was coming and fled in a panic, leaving the lamp alight, or maybe he stumbled in the dark and the lamp overturned. Why hadn't he raised the alarm, though? We could all have been killed! The more I thought about it, the angrier I grew.

Yet outside the shop, I stopped, wondering if confronting Mr Tarver was the right thing to do. Should I go straight to PC Dawes with the whistle? But what if it belonged to Mr Williams? That had to be a possibility. I had to give Mr Tarver a chance to explain, so I opened the door - and there stood Eunice behind the counter.

'Isobel.' Her face lit up. 'Now how are you all doing?'

I had to answer what seemed like a hundred questions as she weighed out the barley sugars and popped in a couple extra 'on the house'. Mr Tarver was nowhere to be seen and the wait was nerve-racking. At last I managed to ask where he was. 'Gone to the village hall,' Eunice replied. 'He's putting up some notice or other. ARP business, it'll be.'

There was no elderflower cordial so I grabbed the bag of sweets and left. The village hall was close by the church, about a quarter of a mile further into the village. Mr Tarver stood outside in the porch, locking the door, and now my courage nearly failed me; only the thought of Gran and Andreas spurred me on. I *had* to find out what had really happened.

'Mr Tarver? Please may I have a word?'

Isobel's Story

He stared at me suspiciously, jangling the heavy bunch of keys, a bowler hat pushed back on his greasy hair. There was an ARP pin badge in his lapel and an ARP armband over the sleeve of his serge suit; no sign of a whistle, though. 'What about? They don't want some security advice up at the Hall, do they? Bit late for that, I'd have thought.'

So he was going to bluster it out. 'Does this belong to you?' I asked, holding up the whistle by its chain. 'I've just found it. In what's left of Lord Vye's studio.'

It might have been my imagination but I could have sworn he stiffened; at any rate, his eyes narrowed, locked on mine. He didn't speak for a few seconds and I thought he was about to deny the whistle was his. But then he said, 'Well, I've been wondering for weeks where that had got to. I knew the lad must have pinched it.' In the blink of an eye, the whistle was out of my grasp and swallowed up in his chubby fingers.

I hadn't thought of that. 'Incriminating evidence, wouldn't you say?' Mr Tarver was obviously enjoying my dismay. 'Perhaps we should hand this in to PC Dawes.'

But of course Andreas wouldn't steal anything, least of all Mr Tarver's whistle. What use was that to him? 'Perhaps we should,' I countered. 'Then I can tell him what I saw that night.'

'What? What did you see?' The words were out

before Mr Tarver could hold them back. We both knew he'd given himself away.

'I saw you on your bicycle, riding up to the Hall in the middle of the night,' I lied, not taking my eyes off his. He wasn't to know I was bluffing, was he?

Now the mask dropped. 'Listen to me, young lady,' he snarled, taking hold of my arm. 'I don't have to answer to you or anyone else in this village when I'm on official duty. There are matters of national security at stake and you'd do as well to keep your mouth shut or you could end up in a great deal of trouble. You and the ... boy.' He spat out the word.

'Nancy nearly died in that fire!' I was too angry to let him intimidate me. 'Andreas is in hospital and my granny's seriously ill. Don't you care?'

He pushed me back against the notice board. 'I'll only say this once. The fire had nothing to do with me. Do you understand? If you start spreading rumours about what you thought you saw, I shall go to the police and tell them things about your young German friend that'll have him sent back where he came from quicker than you can say knife.' A drop of his spittle landed on my cheek. 'And who do you think they're going to believe? A man of good character who's lived in this village twenty years, or some little guttersnipe from London and a Jewboy?'

I couldn't help crying on the way back: tears of anger and frustration. How could I ever have thought myself a match for Mr Tarver? He'd outwitted me on every count and now I'd lost the evidence to prove his guilt. I should have gone to PC Dawes in the first place. Then again, Mr Tarver was right; the police would never take my word over his and Andreas would have ended up in more trouble. I'd only made everything worse.

The toot of a horn interrupted these gloomy thoughts as I approached the Swallowcliffe gates. 'Can I give you a lift, dear?' Mrs Hathaway sat behind the wheel of a small, very untidy motor-car, calling to me through the open window. 'I've come to visit your grandmother. My son says she's out of any immediate danger.'

She talked about nothing for the rest of the way up the drive, tactfully ignoring my red eyes. When we'd parked by the front door, though (in a flurry of gravel), she patted my hand and said, 'This must be a very anxious time for you. If there's anything I can do to help, will you let me know? I'm fond of Polly and her family.'

I nodded, climbing quickly out of the car. It *was* an anxious time, I thought, waiting outside Gran's bedroom while Mum and Mrs Hathaway murmured together inside. Life was rushing past at breakneck speed - Gran turning into an invalid, the Hall being abandoned, war getting closer with each passing day - and there didn't seem much I could do about any of it. Mr Tarver had pointed out how powerless I was. All I could do was sit there, waiting to be told what would happen next. Well, now it was time to think for myself. I put Mr Tarver out of my head for the time being - Andreas was the one to talk to about this - and concentrated on Ralph Chadwick. How could we let him simply walk out of our lives, knowing who he was? I had discovered this secret, and Mum had no right to decide for me what was to be done with it.

Which was why I found myself in the passenger seat of Mrs Hathaway's motor-car that afternoon, being driven up to London. I'd told her in the morning about trying to buy some elderflower cordial for Gran, and she'd said she was driving up to London later that day so she could easily stop by Fortnum and Mason, who were bound to have it. She looked a little surprised when I waylaid her on the way out of Gran's room and asked if I could come too, to help with the shopping, but she didn't seem to mind. 'Of course. I'd be glad of the company and a change of scene would probably do you good. Let's see what your mother thinks about the idea.'

Mum said it was fine with her, as long as I helped make Gran's room in the gate lodge ready that morning; Dr Hathaway would be coming in the afternoon to move her down, but they could manage between the two of them. So Mrs Hathaway picked me up from the lodge early that afternoon, and off we went.

'Ah, the open road,' she said, adjusting a pair

Isobel's Story

of round sunglasses with white frames which looked a little strange with her tweed suit and leather gloves. 'Nothing like setting off on a journey with the wind at your back and the sun on your face. Got your gas mask, dear?'

She drove fast, tooting as we approached every corner. 'Might as well let the enemy know we're coming. Help yourself to a travel sweetie, by the way.' And she waved towards the glove compartment. 'You look a little pale.'

After a while, I decided there was no point holding on to the seat; this was an adventure and I might as well make the most of it. 'So, have you enjoyed your time at Swallowcliffe?' Mrs Hathaway asked, turning her white goggle eyes on me for longer, surely, than was safe.

'Oh, it's been marvellous. Being with Gran, and getting to know the house ... I can't bear to think of it locked up and empty.'

'Sad, isn't it?' Mrs Hathaway tore off one glove with her teeth and leant across me to scrabble in the tin of sweeties, sending a cloud of powdered sugar over the floor. 'The place has changed so much since I was a girl. It was the death duties that crippled us, you know. First my brother Edward getting himself drowned on the *Lusitania*, and then his poor son Charles driving off the road like that.' She made dying sound nothing more than an unfortunate mistake. 'Lionel does his best, but he doesn't have much of a business brain. He'd sooner live in a hut in the South of France and paint all day. And his wife has no idea, really.'

We were veering towards the middle of the road. 'All right, all right,' Mrs Hathaway muttered as an oncoming car swerved past, hooting. 'In my day, the mistress of the house had a sense of responsibility,' she went on, crunching the sweet between her teeth. 'My stepmother might have been a tartar but she always knew if anyone on the estate had fallen ill. The servants were looked after, right till the end.'

That was what Mum hated, though, having to be obliged to the Vyes; she didn't want to accept their help. And they hadn't looked after everyone, had they? Before I could stop myself, the words were out of my mouth. 'Mrs Hathaway, did you know my granny's friend, Iris Baker?'

She shot me another long, dangerous look. 'As it happens, I did. And what have you heard about her, may I ask?'

Now I wished I'd kept quiet. 'Only that she died,' I muttered. 'And that she'd had a baby.'

'Yes, she did, I'm afraid. Now hold on to your hat!' She stepped on the accelerator and the engine roared as we overtook a tractor on the brow of the hill. I closed my eyes as the motor-car lurched out. 'Just made it,' Mrs Hathaway announced cheerfully as we coasted down the other side. 'The thing about

Isobel's Story

Iris,' she continued, 'was that she broke the rules. Servants had to know their place, you see. It was different for me and your granny because we met when I was a girl. Children and staff were treated pretty much the same: we were meant to be seen but not heard. Mind you, both of us learned a lot that way.' She flexed her hands on the steering wheel. 'I've often thought about Iris. By the time I thought to ask the housekeeper where she'd gone, it was too late. She and the baby had died together in the workhouse.'

I gazed at her, wondering how she'd react if she knew about the letter in my coat pocket. It would be such a relief to talk to someone! 'What is it?' she asked. 'I can tell there's something on your mind. Spit it out, dear, and you'll feel a great deal better.'

'The baby didn't die,' I blurted. 'Gran took him away and he was adopted. He's a grown-up man and I've met him. That's why I wanted to come to London, to let him know about his mother.'

With a screech of brakes, Mrs Hathaway brought the car to a sudden halt in the middle of the road. Luckily there was nothing coming behind us. 'What did you say?'

'Iris's son,' I repeated. 'He's alive. His name is Ralph Chadwick. Gran talked about him when she was delirious and then I remembered meeting him. He came to look around the house because he stayed at Swallowcliffe in the war.'

'Good God!' She stared at me. 'And do you know where he lives?'

'No, I don't - apart from the fact that it's somewhere in Scotland.' That had seemed an insoluble problem until another little snippet of information about the Chadwicks had suddenly come back to me. 'He and his wife were staying at the Ritz, though, so they must have his address. I've written to tell him my granny knew his mother and he should get in touch if he wanted to find out about her. I thought he ought to know.'

'I agree.' Mrs Hathaway started up the car again and we drove slowly off. 'And have you told him where to contact you?'

'I gave him the Swallowcliffe address and our London one, in case we've gone home by the time he replies.'

'I want to ask you something,' she said. 'If this letter does reach Mr Chadwick and he replies, will you tell me straight away? It's extremely important.'

'Of course. But the only thing is, my mother told me not to try and find him. She thinks it's better to leave the past alone. Can you keep my part in this a secret?' I bit my lip, wondering if we really were doing the right thing. Mum would be furious if she found out.

'We *must* look for the man.' Mrs Hathaway put a hand on my arm, obviously sensing my doubts. 'There is a great deal more at stake than you realise.'

Chapter Sixteen

Well, if I have to stay here, I shall go completely down the drain. Only work, dirty work. Nothing to learn. I have been to visit Miss Perilman (an acquaintance)... She, like everyone else, keeps telling us how well off we are. No one seems to realise what is happening.

From the diary of Edith Brown-Jacobowitz, a Jewish refugee living in Ireland, 29 June 1939

IT WAS THE MOST MARVELLOUS afternoon. I might have lived in London but Piccadilly wasn't exactly my stamping ground, so everything was new to me. Mrs Hathaway parked the motor-car in a side street and we went to Fortnum's first for the elderflower cordial. Of course it was there, along with every other kind of syrup, juice, tea, chocolate or coffee you could imagine. The cheese counter alone was three times the length of Mr Tarver's whole shop, and as for the display of cakes and biscuits - I'd never seen anything like it in my life.

'I was going to suggest we took tea here,' Mrs Hathaway told me, 'but in view of our mission, perhaps we should stroll along to the Ritz instead.' For this was the most wonderfully convenient thing: the hotel was about five minutes' walk from Fortnum and Mason.

If I'd been on my own, the Ritz might have been too much for me, despite the fact I was wearing the red crêpe frock and court shoes. Even the doorman had gold frogging all over his sleeves and looked like a prince. Under a glittering chandelier, sophisticated people chatted in discreet corners or sauntered past us arm in arm down the long carpeted corridors.

'Darling! How long has it been?' A lady with dazzlingly pale skin and a perfect Cupid's bow mouth under an upturned saucer hat brushed past us to proffer a cheek to her friend.

'Too long, Augusta!' came the reply as they embraced - very carefully, so as not to smudge the lipstick.

'To business first, I think,' said Mrs Hathaway, tucking her arm through mine and marching me forward. 'Do you have the letter to hand?'

She leant one elbow on the Reception desk as a man in tails glided towards us. 'May I help you, madam?' He raised one eyebrow superciliously.

Isobel's Story

'I certainly hope so.' There wasn't a tremor of doubt in her voice. 'We urgently need to contact a certain Mr Ralph Chadwick, who stayed at your hotel a couple of months past.' I gave her the envelope. 'Would you make sure this letter reaches him at the first available opportunity?' She slid it across the desk, with a ten-shilling note tucked discreetly behind.

'Very good, madam,' said the man smoothly, palming the money. 'I'm sure that will present no difficulty.'

'I should hope not,' she replied. 'My father, Lord Vye, used to entertain here often. This is an urgent and important matter, young man. Mr Chadwick may learn something to his advantage, as I believe the expression is, so I'm sure you'll do your best to see he gets the letter right away.'

Some people might have taken Mrs Hathaway for a country bumpkin, in her rumpled tweed suit, stout shoes and a shapeless hat jammed anyhow on her head, but she tackled the Ritz Hotel with perfect confidence. 'Now, Isobel, time for tea.'

And what a tea it was! We stowed our gas masks under the gilt chairs and ate until we were bursting. Tiny cucumber sandwiches on bread so thin you could see though it, scones with jam and clotted cream, a three-tier silver stand piled high with cream cakes and pastries, slices of chocolate cake, seed cake, and a Dundee that was nearly as good as Gran's. Endless tea to drink, of course, in bone china cups with gold rims.

'Good to see a girl with a healthy appetite,' Mrs Hathaway said, helping herself to another *éclair* as we talked. I felt quite at ease in her company, perhaps because she was so at ease with herself. She told me all sorts of things about life at Swallowcliffe before the war, and then more about the house being turned into a hospital. 'Your son fought at the Front, didn't he?' I asked shyly.

'For a year or so,' she replied. 'Then he was invalided out. Needed an emergency op to remove his appendix and the scar meant he couldn't wear an ammunition belt. Funny how one's life can hang on a tiny twist of fate, isn't it? Anyway, he went back to helping me run the hospital after that and we were jolly glad to have him.'

So that was why Mum had written to Dr Hathaway at the Hall. I turned the information over in my mind, thinking about her letters, still in my suitcase. It even crossed my mind to tell Mrs Hathaway about them, but only for one fleeting second; that was a private matter. To change the subject, I started talking about Andreas and the *Kindertransporte*, and how at one time I'd hoped the Vyes might have taken in more refugees at the Hall. 'Poor souls,' Mrs Hathaway said thoughtfully. 'They must be at their wits' end to send those children away.'

Isobel's Story

At last it was time to go. Mrs Hathaway paid the bill, we gathered up our things and went off to find the car. The journey home passed mostly in companionable silence. I felt pleased to have done something at last, and only the tiniest bit worried our mission would turn out to be a mistake. 'Give my love to your granny,' Mrs Hathaway called, when we arrived at the gate lodge. 'And remember, let me know *at once* if you know who gets in touch.' She fished around on the floor of the car, coming up with a library ticket and a pencil stub. 'Here's my phone number.' She scrawled on the ticket and gave it to me. 'There's a telephone box in the village. Promise you'll ring me straight away? I can be over in two shakes of a lamb's tail.'

'Of course,' I said, waving goodbye. 'And thank you for the tea. It was wonderful!'

Mum was washing up at the kitchen sink when I came in through the back door. She smiled when she saw me. 'Izzie! Now we're all together. The boys are playing out in the field and Gran's in the front room. Why don't you pop in and say hello? I think she's awake.'

That morning we'd pushed back the armchairs and made up a single bed which Mr Oakes had brought down from upstairs. (I did wonder how he and Mrs Oakes felt about moving up to the big house, but he seemed his usual implacable self.) Gran was sitting up in it, gazing out of the window on to the drive. She looked rather wan, but a great deal better than she had the day before. 'I've been having such strange dreams, dear,' she said, when I came in. 'And now here I am, back in my old home. Would you believe it?'

'Are you happy, Gran?' I asked.

'Happy as a sandboy,' she said, and I could see from her eyes it was true. 'My family around me, lying here like a queen - I couldn't ask for anything more.'

We were all happy, those next few days. The sun seemed to shine every day and the boys stayed outside from dawn till dusk. They'd go up to the Hall, call at the blue door for Tristan and spend the whole day playing football or making a den somewhere. Tristan was delighted because he didn't have to go back to his horrible prep school any more; he told Stan that he'd be starting the summer term at a new school closer by, where he could come home at the weekends. Nancy was improving every day in hospital, too. One afternoon I went back there to visit Andreas (telling Mum I was going shopping). His face was much better and he was dressed and out of bed, so we could sit in the visitors' day room. I told him what I'd found in the studio, and what Mr Tarver had said about it.

'I knew it! He was looking in there to make trouble for me.' Yet he didn't sound as angry as I'd expected.

Isobel's Story

'What do you think we should do?' I asked. 'I don't have the whistle any more but maybe we should speak to PC Dawes anyway. We can't let Mr Tarver get off scot free.'

'No, you must not do anything. Please!' Now he was agitated. 'Mr Tarver is a dangerous man, I know this. If we say anything against him, it will turn out bad for me. The policeman has not come again and Lord Vye has visited me. He does not think the fire is my fault.' His eyes lit up. 'He came with his aunt, Mrs Hathaway, and they asked about my mother. They will speak to people and try to bring her here. My cousin, too.'

'But that's marvellous!' Good old Mrs Hathaway. She was the kind of person who got things done.

'She tells me you talk with her. Thank you, Isobel. All these things you do for me.' Now I was blushing red as a beetroot. 'I come out of hospital in two days and Lord Vye says I can work as his secretary until my burns are quite better. Write letters for him and such things. Will you be there?'

My heart sank. 'Not for long. Mum says we have to go home at the end of the week. Gran needs looking after so she's coming with us. But I'll see you before we go.'

It felt all wrong, taking Gran away from Swallowcliffe. We were so snug in the gate lodge, I couldn't help imagining what life would be like if we never went back to London. Alfie would go to the village primary, while Stan and I would catch the bus into Edenvale where there was bound to be a senior school for us. Mum would lose the frown lines between her eyes and maybe she'd actually start being nice to Dr Hathaway instead of looking at him as though he was about to sprout another head. Gran would get better and Hitler would realise there was no point in going to war.

And pigs would fly. 'Of course we can't stay here, it's out of the question,' Mum snapped when I raised the subject that evening at supper. 'London is our home. It's where my job is, and where you and the boys go to school. We can't stay here on sufferance any longer.'

I had one last try. 'But we could find other schools, and maybe you could find another job. We could even rent this house from the Vyes, perhaps. Don't you want to come back here, Mum?'

'No, I do not.' She started to clear the plates. 'There's nothing here for us. Now go and fetch your granny's tray.'

Gran hadn't drunk much of her soup. 'Don't waste your breath,' she said, patting my hand as I reached for the bowl. 'It's like banging your head against a brick wall, trying to change her mind.'

'You don't want to come to London, though, do you?' I asked.

'Oh, that's not going to happen,' she said, closing

Isobel's Story

her eyes. 'I'm afraid you'll have to go without me.'

They were both as stubborn as each other, and I couldn't see how the situation would resolve itself. Early the next morning, Dr Hathaway called in to see how Gran was and talked to Mum afterwards in the kitchen about the idea of moving her. I sat on the stairs, listening to them through the open door. 'Look, Grace,' he said, 'I'm not trying to keep you here. I just don't think a long journey is the best thing for your mother at the moment. Can't you leave her where she is for a little longer?'

'The children have to go back to school, and so do I,' Mum replied obstinately. 'Once I get Ma home, I'll be able to look after her - my neighbour can pop in during the day and we'll all be there in the evening. Who's going to take care of her here? She needs to be with her family and we need to be in London, there's no way round it. Anyway, you said yourself how much better she was.'

'She might be better but the fever's left her very weak.' He lowered his voice; I had to crane forward to hear. It sounded something like, 'not as much time as you think'.

'You know my mother's tough as old boots,' Mum said. 'She'll outlive us all.'

'Well, if your mind's set on it, at least let me drive you there.' There was a pause and he burst out, 'Come on, Grace! She can hardly go on the train.'

'No, I suppose not. Thank you, Philip. That's

very good of you.'

At least she was calling him by his Christian name, but it wasn't an encouraging conversation. This was our future: none of us would ever come back to the Hall, Mum would never see Dr Hathaway again, and Gran would be miserable in London for the rest of her life.

'Isobel? I'm just popping off to the shop,' Mum called a little later when the doctor had gone. (Luckily she enjoyed going off to the village; I couldn't bear the thought of encountering Mr Tarver and came up with every excuse under the sun to avoid the shopping.) 'Listen out for Granny, won't you?'

I took my mug and went to sit outside on the bench that was built into the house, next to the front door. This must have been where a servant would have waited to open the gates if a carriage was expected. These days, the gates stayed open all the time. Some time afterwards, a taxi inched through them with a passenger in the back. Shading my eyes from the sun, I looked at him; he was staring straight ahead and didn't notice me. Just as the car drove past, he leant forward to speak to the driver and I got a better glimpse of his face. And promptly poured my tea all down my front. The passenger in the taxi was Ralph Chadwick.

'Gran, there's something I need to talk to you about.'
She was up and dressed in a skirt and cardigan,

Isobel's Story

sitting in a chair by the window. 'Come on in, then,' she said. 'Don't be shy.'

My heart was thumping. She still looked so frail, the skin sunken between her collarbones and the neck of the jersey gaping, her bony wrists sticking out of the sleeves. Was Mum right? Would this shock be too much? I'd been expecting Ralph Chadwick to write back to me, not turn up without any warning; I could have shown Gran his letter and she would have had time to decide whether she wanted to see him. But here he was in person, and he'd be coming back down to the gate lodge as soon as he found out where we were. I had to prepare her.

'It's to do with your friend, Iris Baker,' I said, kneeling by Gran's chair. 'Remember when you showed me her grave? Well, when you were ill, you said something about her baby.'

'Did I, indeed?' She raised her eyebrows. 'And what did you make of that?'

I decided to stick to the bones of the matter. 'The thing was, you mentioned his name. It was Ralph. Ralph Chadwick, wasn't it?' She didn't reply, but I pressed on regardless. 'His name rang a bell because the thing is, Gran ...'

'What?' she demanded. 'What *is* this wretched thing? Come on, out with it.'

I took her hand. 'Well, he came to the Hall one day, with his wife. You were resting and I showed them around the house.'

Her fingers tightened around mine. 'No,' she said distantly. 'It's not possible. It couldn't be him. Not Iris's Ralph. Not here, not after all this time.' She narrowed her eyes at me. 'How do you know? What did he tell you? Does he know about her?'

'This Mr Chadwick's father was a vicar not far away,' I said carefully, 'and he stayed at the Hall in the war when it was a hospital but he didn't say anything else about it. Certainly nothing about Iris.'

She sank back in the chair. 'Dear Lord. I thought he must have been killed in the war like all the others. Can it really be true? After so long?'

'He was nice, Gran. He tipped me half a crown.'

She shook her head. 'That little mite! I've prayed for him every day of my life. I smuggled him out of the workhouse, you know, wrapped up in a shawl under my cloak, and took him to my village. Little Rising, it was. But after my mother died I didn't go back to the place so often and then the Chadwicks passed away and nobody could tell me where he was. It had to be kept a secret, you see, because of the family. I didn't tell a soul, not even William.' She seized my hand again. 'It's been eating me up all these years. Where is he, Isobel? Where's Ralph? I have to see him!'

'He's here,' I said. 'Up at the house. I expect he'll be down any minute.'

She didn't sound at all surprised. 'Bring him to

Isobel's Story

me as soon as he arrives.' She leant back and closed her eyes. 'But I should like a drop of brandy from the corner cupboard first. Mr Oakes has kindly left a quarter bottle behind.'

I poured her a small glass and went to wait for our visitor at the front door. Mr Chadwick was not the first to arrive: Mrs Hathaway pipped him to the post, abandoning her motor-car skew-whiff on the grass verge beyond the house. I'd kept my promise and run to the village telephone box to ring her before doing anything else. 'I won't see Polly till after he's been,' she said, installing herself in the kitchen. 'She'll want a little time now to collect her thoughts.'

I started to fill the kettle. 'Let's hope the shock won't be too much for her.'

Mrs Hathaway flapped a hand dismissively. 'Don't you worry. It'd take more than a minor commotion like this to knock our Polly off her stride.'

The time crawled past as we waited, sitting opposite each other at the table. I was praying Mum wouldn't arrive first; it was too much to hope that Mr Chadwick would have come and gone by the time she came back from the village. Then at last we heard a knock on the front door and there they were: Mr Chadwick and Dr Hathaway. 'I was up at the Hall, seeing Lionel,' he said, 'so I thought I'd bring this gentleman down myself. I believe you know each other.'

'Isobel? I came as soon as I could.' Mr Chadwick held out his hand. 'Thank you for your letter. We have a lot to talk about.'

I remembered his open, honest face - particularly the piercing blue eyes - but knowing he was Iris Baker's son made it even more appealing. Shaking his hand felt like reaching back into the past, to a time when Gran had been young and the Hall was in its heyday.

'It's my granny you need to talk to. She knows you're coming.' I hesitated. 'She's been ill, though, like I said in my letter.'

'It's all right,' he said. 'I won't stay long. As soon as she seems tired, I'll leave.'

Mrs Hathaway was lurking in the kitchen doorway. 'Show him in,' she said. 'Then we'll all introduce each other afterwards.'

I opened the door to the front room but Mr Chadwick walked through on his own. This was a private moment, it seemed to me; Gran wouldn't have wanted an audience. The Hathaways and I went into the kitchen and made conversation to show we weren't eavesdropping. 'Do you know what all this is about?' Dr Hathaway asked his mother. 'Sounds very mysterious. I thought I'd better stay to make sure Mrs Stanbury's all right.'

'Two words,' she replied significantly. 'Iris Baker.' I could tell the name meant something to him, but at that very moment the back door opened and Mum came in.

'What is it?' She looked at each of us in turn. 'You're all very serious. Is there something I should know?' And then, as she heard the voices, 'Who's that talking to Ma?'

'It's Ralph Chadwick,' I told her. 'He came back.'

Her shopping basket fell on the floor. 'Oh, Isobel! You silly girl! What *have* you gone and done?'

Chapter Seventeen

I have little doubt that Hitler knows quite well that we mean business. The only question to which he is not sure of the answer is whether we mean to attack him as soon as we are strong enough. If he thought we did, he would naturally argue that he had better have the war when it suits him than wait until it suits us.
Prime Minister Neville Chamberlain, July 1939

'THE ISSUE WE'RE SO delicately skirting around,' said Mrs Hathaway, resting both hands flat on the table, 'is not so much Mr Chadwick's mother as his father. Who happens to be Edward Vye, my older brother. The sixth Lord Vye, Lionel's father,' she added for my benefit.

Dr Hathaway spluttered over a mouthful of tea. 'Good Lord.'

Isobel's Story

'You knew all along!' Mum stared at her. 'How? I thought I was the only one who'd found out.'

'Thirteen-year-old girls take in a lot more than people give them credit for,' Mrs Hathaway said. 'I had my suspicions at the time, so a few years later I asked the housekeeper. She was a sensible woman, Mrs Henderson, and she knew I'd be discreet. It was dreadful, what happened to Iris. Made me ashamed to be part of the family.'

'With good reason.' The sharpness in Mum's voice had me wincing, but Mrs Hathaway didn't seem to notice.

'By that time it was too late to help the poor girl,' she went on, 'but we ought to do right by her son. He and Lionel are half-brothers, after all. He doesn't have any claim on the title, being illegitimate, but he ought to have a stake in the house.'

'But we can't let Ma find out!' Mum spoke in a fierce whisper. 'She adored Lord Vye - Edward Vye, I mean - worshipped the ground he walked on. If she learned he was the father of Iris's baby, it would kill her. That's why I didn't want you raking up the past, Isobel. Why couldn't you listen to me for once?'

'Because I thought she'd want to see him,' I protested. 'And surely Mr Chadwick should know who his mother and father were. Why do we have the right but not him?'

'Don't be so impertinent.' She glared at me. 'I'm only thinking of Gran. She mustn't be upset, especially not now.'

I jumped up from the table. 'Then don't go dragging her off to London when she doesn't want to go, just because it suits you!'

As soon as the words were out of my mouth, I knew I'd gone too far. Mum flushed with anger. 'Go to your room at once,' she said in an icy voice. 'And don't come down until you're prepared to apologise for such appalling behaviour.'

She was quite justified: I had been unforgivably rude. I just couldn't bear the way she kept lecturing me, as though she were the only one who knew what was best for Gran. I was certain Gran would want to see Ralph Chadwick as much as anyone in the world, and she had. What I'd have given to be a fly on the wall during that conversation! A hum of voices drifted up from downstairs. I was too embarrassed to venture out and sat glumly on the edge of the bed, wondering what was happening below.

Half an hour or so later, I heard Mr Chadwick emerge from the front room. From what I could make out, the Hathaways were going to take him back up to the Hall. Perhaps they were planning to introduce him to Lord Vye? Eventually the front door slammed behind them and the house was quiet. It took another couple of hours, though, before I could summon the courage to go downstairs and say sorry.

Mum was scrubbing the oven with Vim, her

hair tied up in a flowery headscarf. 'I should think so!' She sat back on her heels. 'In front of the Hathaways, too. I was ashamed of you, Isobel - there's no other word for it. What on earth possessed you?'

I tried to explain. 'You made me feel so awful. I love Gran too, Mum, and I sort of understand how she feels about Swallowcliffe. Of course I shouldn't have put it like that, but I really don't feel we ought to take her to London if there's any way round it. No matter how much you hate being beholden to the Vyes.'

'You deliberately disobeyed me! I told you not to try and find Ralph Chadwick and you went right ahead and did it. Goodness knows how.' She went back to the oven, her arm flying to and fro like a piston as tiny flecks of Vim paste splattered the kitchen floor. 'You should have left well alone. How do you think Gran's going to feel when she learns she's been wrong about Iris all her life?'

I couldn't see that mattered so much, not compared with the joy of seeing Iris's son, but Mum didn't wait for an answer. Abruptly, she threw the scouring cloth into the sink and peeled off her rubber gloves. 'But I've had a talk with Dr Hathaway and he thinks much the same. So I've written to the school, asking for two weeks' emergency leave. I can set the boys some work to do here and you'll just have to study by yourself. And I'll be paying the Vyes rent, so everything's fair and square. Don't think it's anything to do with your little outburst, though,' she added darkly. 'Speak to me like that again and you'll have your bottom spanked, big as you are.'

'Yes, Mum.' I backed out of the room, careful to sound penitent rather than triumphant. Thank goodness! Gran would be staying here for a while and so would we; there might even be a chance to find out how the story with Ralph Chadwick would unfold. 'Can I see Gran now?' I asked from the doorway.

'Not for the minute. She's resting and I don't want her disturbed. You can take yourself off somewhere - see if Mrs Oakes has anything for you to do. There's a pasty on the table for your dinner.'

I set off up the drive with my pasty wrapped in greaseproof paper and an apple, feeling I'd got off lightly. Sunshine was turning the blades of grass into so many shiny emerald needles and I couldn't bear the idea of going straight to Mrs Oakes and doing housework. Instead, I skirted the house and climbed up to sit on the bench at the bottom of the Fairview Tower. There'd be such a lot to tell Andreas when I next saw him! Maybe Lord Vye was right about destiny. It seemed to me that Ralph Chadwick was meant to come to the Hall at this particular time, even though I'd stepped in to bring it about - just like Gran smuggling baby Ralph out of the workhouse. Two little figures were walking along the terrace, far below. It was difficult to tell for sure from this

Isobel's Story

distance, but I thought Lord Vye might have been showing his newly found half-brother around the grounds.

I walked on for ages through the fields, looking for a good spot to eat my picnic and thinking about life. Mum didn't really care whether I helped Mrs Oakes or not, she only wanted me out from under her feet, so I didn't feel guilty about pleasing myself all afternoon and going straight back to the gate lodge in the early evening. The boys were weeding the front garden and Mum was nowhere to be seen. Quietly, I opened the door to Gran's room. She'd gone to bed in a fleecy bedjacket, but she wasn't asleep.

'Izzie! I've been waiting for you.' She patted the bed. 'Come here and talk to me.'

'Was it all right, Gran?' I bent over her. 'Seeing Mr Chadwick, I mean.'

'Better than that. We had such a wonderful talk, dear. I told him all about her.'

I started to pull over a chair from the window, but it was a heavy old thing. 'Leave that,' Gran said, patting the mattress. 'There's plenty of room here. Kick off your shoes and lie next to me where I can see you properly. I've something to show you.'

When I was settled, she held out a silver locket. 'This was my mother's. When you press this button on the top, it opens up. See?' Inside was a photograph of a girl with a frilly servant's cap perched on her fair hair. 'That's Iris.' Gran passed me the locket for a closer look. 'Wasn't she lovely?'

I stared at the small picture. There was such an arresting expression on Iris's face: bold and wary at the same time, as if her mouth couldn't help smiling but her eyes knew the danger. 'Ralph brought the locket with him,' Gran said, 'so I'd know he was the one. It was my mother's. I put in Iris's picture and left it with Mrs Chadwick all those years ago so he could see what his own mother looked like.' She closed my fingers over the silver frame. 'I want Grace to have this when I'm gone, and then it will come to you. Give Ralph the photograph, though.'

'Oh, Gran! Don't even talk about it.' I passed the locket back to her and arranged the coverlet snugly over my legs. 'Are you sure you've got enough room?'

'Plenty.' There was hardly anything of her under the blankets.

I gazed out of the window. The sky was quite beautiful: a pale milky blue with marshmallow clouds flushed pink and gold from the setting sun. Gran stroked my hair. 'Dear Isobel,' she said softly. 'You've been a great blessing to me.'

'And vice versa.' I wanted her to know that. 'We're lucky, aren't we?'

'I should say so.'

It was so comfortable, lying there, that my eyes began to close; Gran was dozing, too. The sky gradually turned darker, swallowing up the clouds. 'Listen!' she said at one point, turning her face towards the window. I could hear a twittering, squeaking sound as dozens of black arrows darted about the house eaves, swirling though the velvety dusk. 'The swallows are here.' Gran smiled at me. 'Summer's coming.'

I watched them with a wonderful sense of contentment. We were all together, and safe, and everything would turn out fine. A short while later, some instinct made me turn to Gran. Her head was slumped forward a little on her chest and she didn't look comfortable.

'Are you all right?' I asked, adjusting the pillow behind her.

'Perfectly,' she whispered, but her voice was very faint and now her breathing was beginning to sound strange, irregular. I sat up, wondering if I should call Mum.

There was no time. Gran suddenly raised herself and looked past me into the depths of the room, her eyes shining with joy and one hand lifted a few inches, still holding the locket, as though greeting an old friend she hadn't seen for some time. The next second, all that light and life had left her face. She fell back against the pillow, the locket slithering through her fingers on to the floor, and I knew she was gone. Laying my head against the soft woollen bedjacket, I wept - not for her, but for myself.

Gran's funeral was held at the church in Stone Martin. We sang her favourite hymn, 'Jerusalem', Reverend Murdoch said something about a sense of duty and a life well lived, and then Lord Vye read a lesson from the Bible. Aunt Hannah and Uncle Alf had travelled down from Yorkshire and both the Hathaways were there, along with the Swallowcliffe staff and pretty much the whole village. It was a blessing Mr Tarver didn't turn up. I couldn't have borne to see him, knowing what he'd put Gran through. And Lady Vye was still in London with Tristan and the girls; they were staying with the Gordon-Smythes until the Dower House was ready. Andreas came, though, wearing a special cotton glove to protect his left hand. I saw a few people turn around to stare at him as he took a seat near the back of the church. His face looked much better but the mark of the fire was still on it, and perhaps always would be.

After the service, we trooped along to the village hall for refreshments. I stood pouring endless cups of tea, lost in a fug of misery. It was impossible to believe Gran had gone. I'd never be able to talk to her again, never share with her the good things and the bad that would happen in my life, never have her warm smile to comfort me.

'I'm so sorry, Isobel.' Dr Hathaway was holding out two cups for a refill. 'I've known your grandmother since I was a child. We shall all miss

Isobel's Story

her enormously.'

I put down the teapot. 'May I speak to you for a moment, privately?' The thought had been tormenting me that I could have been responsible for Gran's death; that if I hadn't brought Ralph Chadwick back to the Hall, she might still be alive. We found a quiet corner and I asked the question, dreading what he might say.

Dr Hathaway considered it seriously. 'To be honest, I think she could have gone at any time. She was very weak. But I saw her after Mr Chadwick had left and she seemed peaceful rather than agitated.' He put an arm around my shoulder as we walked back to the throng. 'Sometimes people need permission to die. I had the feeling your grandmother's mind had been put at rest, and that counts for a lot.'

I wasn't sure Mum saw it that way, though. We hadn't talked properly yet and her face was as closed as a shop with the shutters down. Mr Chadwick had offered his condolences at the church gate and she'd hardly acknowledged him. She probably blamed him a little, but me most of all. Ralph Chadwick was still with us; he'd taken a room at the village pub and he was up at the Hall every day, talking to Lord Vye and Andreas, and the Hathaways too. He'd written me the most extraordinary letter. I re-read it each night before I went to sleep, but it was still hard to take in.

Swallowcliffe Hall

25 April 1939

Dear Isobel

We have met only twice and I hesitate to write to you at such a painful time, but I very much wanted you to know the difference you and your grandmother have made to my life. I had always wondered about my natural mother: who she was, and the circumstances which led to her giving me up. Being able to speak to someone who knew and loved her was a great privilege, and the joy of discovering I have a family is beyond words.

I was shocked to hear of your grandmother's death so soon after our conversation, and offer my deepest condolences to you and your mother. I should very much have liked to have told Mrs Stanbury of the plan we have come up with - the Hathaways, Lord Vye and myself. (He and I have decided to refer to each other as distant cousins, to limit the inevitable gossip!) I have felt strongly drawn to Swallowcliffe Hall since my convalescence here during the war. Lord Vye tells me the house is too large for his family, too much of a burden, and of course it would be far too big for Dotty and me to live in alone now our children are grown. But I have a plan to put the Hall to good use once again - a plan that may sound familiar to you.

Isobel's Story

In a nutshell, we should like to turn the house into a boarding school for refugee children, run by me and my wife. I used to be a teacher and, frankly, I'm finding retirement a little dull. We have asked the Baldwin Fund and the Refugee Children's Movement for help with renovations, I have a small income myself, and Mrs Hathaway is busy raising more money. Andreas is proving an invaluable translator, and we trust his mother can act as housekeeper in due course as Mrs Oakes feels this role would be too much at her time of life. So we are well on the way!

I hope your grandmother would have approved. What would Iris have thought, I wonder, of her son taking over the reins at Swallowcliffe? Perhaps they are both looking down on us. Kindly, I hope.

With the deepest thanks and sincerest sympathies,

Ralph Chadwick

I hadn't been able to speak to Andreas about any of this. There was no reason for me to go up to the Hall now, and on the couple of occasions when I'd been able to give Mum the slip and go for a walk, he'd been busy with Lord Vye. He was with him now, and Mr Chadwick. I caught sight of Eunice watching them too, and could imagine what she was thinking: Andreas had managed to 'worm his way in' at last. But he'd saved Nancy's life and had the scars to prove it! Lord Vye was bound to be grateful.

As if he could sense my gaze, he looked over, and the next minute, he was beside me. 'Isobel, I am so sorry for you. It is a very sad thing. Are you all right?'

I didn't want to look at him. All through the funeral, I'd managed not to cry, but something about his face, so concerned and - I had to admit - so dear, threatened to undo my self-control. Apart from my family, no one else in that room mattered half as much to me as he did. What was the good of it, though? Our link with Swallowcliffe had gone; now I really did have to go home and he would be embarking on a new life I'd know nothing about. We'd made friends because he was lonely, that was all, and soon he wouldn't be lonely any more. 'I shall miss her,' I said. 'But you know what that's like.'

He touched my cheek with his fingers, just for an instant. 'If there's anything -'

'Isobel, you've done your duty now.' Mum was walking over to interrupt us, very elegant and cold in her tight black frock and veiled hat. 'Could you take the boys home, please?' She acknowledged Andreas with a brief nod. 'You should start packing up before long.' We were leaving the next day.

'I wish we didn't have to go,' Alfie complained as we walked back to the gate lodge. 'It's good here.'

Isobel's Story

'Well, we do,' I snapped. 'So you might as well make the best of it.'

We'd been living out of suitcases for so long that packing hardly took a minute. A little while later, Aunt Hannah put her head round the bedroom door. 'Everything all right, Izzie?' Her plump, powdery face was very kind but I couldn't start unburdening myself; she wasn't what you'd call a kindred spirit. So I waited for Mum to come home. We had to talk.

It was well into the afternoon before I saw her, gazing out over the field at the back of the house with her arms folded. She'd changed into an old skirt and jersey, and everything about her seemed unbuttoned, slumped, dejected. When I saw her face, I could tell she'd been crying.

'Mum?' I slipped my arm through hers. 'I'm sorry.'

'Everyone's been saying that today.' She squeezed my hand.

'I'm sorry for what I did, I mean. Bringing Ralph Chadwick to the Hall. You were right - I shouldn't have done it.'

'Oh, that. No, I'm glad you did. It's what Gran would have wanted. I talked to her after he left and she was so happy.' Mum's eyes filled with tears. 'How did you manage to understand her so much better than I ever could?'

I didn't know what to say. 'She was so proud of you. She was always telling everyone how well you'd done, getting trained as a teacher and raising us on your own.'

Mum stared at me blankly. 'Really? I had no idea.'

I lowered my voice. 'Don't let Aunt Hannah or the others find out, but she said to me once that you were her favourite daughter.'

'Oh, Izzie.' Now Mum was crying properly. 'I loved her so much and I never told her. Do you think she knew?'

'Of course she did.' We clung together, weeping for the terrible gap that had been left in our lives, holding on tight for the support that wasn't to be found anywhere else.

'At least we've got each other,' Mum said at last, wiping her nose. 'Goodness, I feel better for that.'

It might have been the perfect moment to show her the letters Gran had entrusted to me. Except I no longer had them. Giving Mum those letters wouldn't make the slightest difference, I knew that; she was too proud to change the path she'd chosen. So I'd handed them to Dr Hathaway in the village hall instead. After all, they had been addressed to him - even if they were more than twenty years late.

We were walking down the garden path, arm in arm, when the sound of hooves and the sight of two horses trotting through the gates brought us to a halt. Dr Hathaway was riding one and leading another alongside by the reins. He'd changed into

Isobel's Story

jodhpurs and a white shirt with the sleeves rolled up, and he looked heart-stoppingly handsome, even though he was so old. 'Grace?' he called. 'I felt in the mood for a gallop and thought you might like to come with me. I warn you, I'm not taking no for an answer.'

She stared at him. 'But I've got nothing to wear. And I haven't been on a horse for twenty years.'

He unhooked a haversack from his back and tossed it over. 'There are breeches and boots in there. You can have five minutes to get ready.'

Mum caught the bag awkwardly. 'I can't take off just like that,' she said, holding it as she might a bomb that was about to explode in her hands. 'There are a thousand and one things to be done.'

'Go on, Mum,' I urged in a whisper. 'None of that boring stuff matters. What are you so afraid of?'

'Briar's very steady, if you're worried about falling off,' Dr Hathaway said sneakily. The second horse tossed its head, a hank of black forelock flopping over one eye. It didn't look very steady to me.

'Oh, that doesn't bother me.' Mum tilted her chin obstinately and met his gaze straight on. 'All right, then. I'll come along, since you're both so set on it. But only for an hour or so.' And she ran into the house to change, looking not much older than me.

'Thank you, Isobel.' He smiled down at me.

'You're welcome,' I said, and it wasn't just a figure of speech.

Gran had tried to keep Mum from getting hurt, but she hadn't needed protection any more than I did now. I set off for the village, to see if Andreas might still be around.

Chapter Eighteen

Ach, ja, now there is nothing to be done. I hope for the best. By the time you receive this letter, everything will have been decided. Never has the writing of a letter been so difficult as today. All the time I am thinking of the good parents. Do I have to give away everything that I love? War is nothing but a small word. All the dead behind it, the death, is dreadful.
From a letter by Edith Brown-Jacobowitz, a Jewish refugee in Ireland, to her uncle, 29 August 1939

IT WAS WELL PAST FIVE by now and the village shop had closed, to my relief. As I walked past, a notice in the window caught my eye. 'Civil Defence meeting, Friday 28 April at 6 p.m. in the Village Hall,' it read, and the word 'TONIGHT' had been added at the top in large red capitals. 'Come and discuss IMPORTANT issues of the day which affect us

ALL. Refreshments provided, courtesy of the W.I.'

There were more of these notices on lampposts and another pinned to the board outside the hall itself. I looked through the window to see all traces of the funeral tea cleared away and the place virtually empty, except for Mr Williams laying out chairs in rows. Andreas must have gone long since. I turned around to go back, and nearly walked straight into Mr Tarver, carrying a cardboard box of leaflets.

He looked about as pleased to see me as I was to see him. 'What are you doing hanging round here? This is village business, it's got nothing to do with you.'

'Mum wanted me to make sure everything's as it should be after the funeral,' I told him coldly.

He didn't bother to offer condolences. 'I hope you haven't forgotten our conversation. Not been blabbing, have you?' Droplets of sweat glistened on his upper lip. I suddenly realised something quite extraordinary. He was afraid of me. Not only that: I was no longer afraid of him.

'The truth will come out in the end,' I said. 'It always does. You've got more to worry about than what I might say, Mr Tarver.'

'Clear off.' He jerked his head. 'Get back to London where you belong. You're not welcome in Stone Martin.'

I did go away, but only around the corner to a bench by the pond. What were he and Mr

Isobel's Story

Williams up to? What was so secret about a meeting in the village hall? It seemed to me that Mr Tarver particularly didn't want me there, which was a good enough reason to make every effort go. I waited until just before six, then retraced my steps to the hall and slipped in behind everyone else to take a seat at the back. There was a leaflet on every chair with a picture of the village green on the front.

'To all residents of Stone Martin,' I read inside. 'URGENT news. A proposal has just come to our knowledge which will change the character of this village for good. Do you want to protect your country's glorious heritage in these dangerous times? Are you concerned about an influx of foreign residents? Then let your voice be heard! For the sake of your family, say NO to the Jewish hostel!'

So that was their game. Mr Tarver and Mr Williams sat up on the platform behind a table wearing their ARP regalia, next to a couple of other men I hadn't seen before. Nearly everyone else in the hall had come to Gran's funeral, and those I didn't know by name, I mostly recognised by sight. Everyone was reading the leaflet with various expressions of bafflement - apart from Eunice, sitting near the front, who had her 'secret' face on. There was a general hum of conversation, until Mr Williams stood up at five past six and banged on the table with a small hammer to declare the meeting open. He introduced the men beside him, one of whom turned out to be a local councillor and the other, a 'colleague' from London, and then he informed us of the shocking proposal to turn our beloved Swallowcliffe Hall into a hostel for Jewish refugees, which they intended to make the main subject for debate.

'Can you imagine the effect of so many foreigners on our small village, let alone the house itself?' he asked, his reedy voice cracking with emotion. 'The Hall has already been damaged by fire in some mysterious "accident". Are we prepared to stand aside and see it destroyed completely? Goodness only knows the mess those people will leave behind.'

Next to him, Mr Tarver mopped his forehead with a handkerchief. How can you sit there and listen to this? I wanted to ask him. Aren't you ashamed?

At last Mr Williams introduced the colleague from London and sat down. It wasn't clear what this man was doing on the platform, but he certainly had a lot to say about the Jewish ghettoes that were ruining London. Jews undercut everybody else by charging cheaper prices, they took jobs from honest working people and food out of their children's mouths, and stealing was part of their nature. It was his duty to warn us, he said, because he could see what would happen in this village, clear as day, and if we didn't take notice of what he said, we'd all be sorry. He had an educated, pleasant voice and he looked the perfect gentleman, standing up on the platform in a three-piece suit with a gold watch chain stretching across his waistcoat front. I wondered whether he was one of Oswald Mosley's lot, even though he wasn't wearing a black shirt.

Then he sat down, and Mr Tarver invited questions or comments from the floor. After a few seconds' silence, Eunice got to her feet. 'It's true, what he says about the jobs and that,' she said. 'I used to work at the Hall and then they got some foreign girl in my place. We don't know anything about these people. Why do they want to come over here? What if they're German spies?' She sat down.

'Anyone else like to comment?' asked Mr Tarver.

Nobody spoke; I think they were all stunned. So I stood up. 'It's not like that at all,' I began. My voice sounded thin and childish. Clearing my throat, I started again. 'You've got it wrong. That's not how it is.' There was a ripple of movement as everybody in the hall turned around to stare; a sea of white faces all looking in my direction, all listening to me.

Mr Tarver was already on his feet, pointing at me. 'This meeting is for residents only. You have no right to contribute.'

I couldn't sit down, my legs seemed incapable of bending, so I stood staring at him like a prize idiot until Mr Prior, the butcher, said, 'Let the lass speak. Her family's been a part of this village for longer than you, Mr Tarver, and certainly longer than your friend on the platform. We should hear what she has to say, today of all days.'

'Hear, hear.' I recognised Miss Hartcup's voice, and it gave me courage.

'The refugees who'd be coming to the Hall are children,' I said. 'They don't want to take the food out of anyone's mouths or do anyone else's job, and they won't steal or make a mess. All they want is somewhere safe to stay because their lives are so terrible under the Nazis.'

'We don't know that for certain, do we?' Eunice had popped up again. 'Why should we take their word for it? They're probably just looking for a chance to start over, better themselves by taking advantage of our hard work and good nature.'

Now Mr Tarver was on his feet. 'I know about that from personal experience,' he said loudly. 'You offer these people Christian charity and they throw it back in your face.'

'But they're children!' I repeated. 'Some of them as young as four or five, and not speaking a word of English. Do you think their parents want to let them go? Can you imagine how desperate they must be, even to think of sending their children away to perfect strangers in a foreign country, not knowing whether they'll ever see them again?' I stopped, suddenly wondering what gave me the right to lecture a room full of adults.

Isobel's Story

'I couldn't do it with mine unless I had to,' said Mrs Olds abruptly, standing up. 'And if I did have to, I should want to know there was some kind soul who'd take them in. I say let them come, poor things, and let's try to make them feel at home.'

'And what happens when they grow up?' asked the man from London in his reasonable voice. 'They might be innocent little children now but they won't stay that way for ever.'

'When it's safe, they'll go home to their families.' I had to make one last appeal. 'We might not be able to stop the war but this is one good thing that at least we can do. I know it's what my grandmother would have wanted, and no one could have loved Swallowcliffe more than she did.'

Now Sissy got up. 'Yes, she would, and I'd agree. I had all sorts of funny ideas about Jews until I got to know one, and then I found out they're not so different from us after all. They're as honest or otherwise as the next man, and that boy Andreas up at the Hall is braver than anyone in this room. Don't you all know he saved Miss Nancy's life? Anyway, Eunice Priddy, you handed in your notice because you didn't want to work at the Hall any more, so don't come over all hard done by now.'

With that, the tide of the meeting had well and truly turned. The more the man from London tried to change everyone's mind, the more unpopular he became. In the end, Mr Tarver and Mr Williams' proposal to table a formal objection to the idea of a home for Jewish refugees was soundly defeated.

'Well done,' Mr Prior told me on the way out. 'I reckon your granny would have been proud.'

The strange thing was, I'd felt Gran very close to me, almost as though she'd been putting the words into my mouth. She knew better than anyone that the Hall was a healing place, and she couldn't have borne to see it left empty. My legs were shaking but I was glad to have spoken out. I still hadn't found Andreas, though, and by now it was getting dark - too dark to walk up to the Hall and bump into him by chance. I went home to the gate lodge and waited for Mum to come back from her ride. Her cheeks were flushed and her eyes sparkling, but that could have been the exercise; she certainly wasn't giving anything away. In fact, she didn't say much for the rest of the evening, although I watched her like a hawk. Aunt Hannah and Uncle Alf had left already because they were breaking the journey with Alf's brother in Birmingham. We had supper together, the boys went to bed and eventually I followed them. Apparently we'd be leaving before I'd had the chance to say goodbye to Andreas. I could hardly believe this was happening, even though we'd said our goodbyes so many times already.

I'd reckoned without him. Early the next morning, I woke to the noise of a hailstorm outside. Could hailstones be quite so loud and scratchy?

Isobel's Story

Wrapping a blanket round my shoulders, I staggered over to the window and looked out. He was standing down below, dark hair spilling over the collar of his jersey and white teeth shining as he smiled up at me, his hand drawn back to throw another shower of pebbles. 'Isobel, come down! We must have a last walk.'

I struggled into some clothes, hastily brushed my teeth without any water and crept down the stairs to meet him. We were both laughing a little to be out so early, with not another soul in the world, as we set off towards the house in the grey, early-morning light. Then he said seriously, 'I am so sorry because of your grandmother. You will miss her very much, I think.'

'Yes, I will. But at least she died here, where she was happy, not miserable in London.' It was amazing how I could talk to him about anything.

'You will not be miserable in London, though. You have your friends there, and lots of studies to do, and I shall write to tell you what happens at Swallowcliffe. Do you know my mother comes here soon?' He took my hand and swung it along in his. 'So many things I must thank you for. Sissy tells me about this meeting last night and what you say. I think there cannot be another girl as Isobel in all of England.'

'So you do like me, then?' I asked shyly. 'I used to think you didn't.'

'But of course I like you,' he said. 'No, I love you! You are the little sister I never had.'

Have you heard the expression, 'the bottom dropped out of my world'? Until then, I'd never really understood what it meant. Now I did. That awful, sinking sense of being cast adrift, of flailing about in search of solid ground beneath your feet and finding none, of not knowing the first thing to do or say.

'Oh, Isobel,' Andreas said gently, seeing my face. 'I'm sorry. I didn't realise.'

'It's all right. I'm fine.' I turned back towards the lodge, burning with shame, hating myself for being so young and stupid. How could I possibly have fallen in love with someone who thought of me as his little sister? Why hadn't I realised that Andreas would never look at me in the way Dr Hathaway looked at Mum? My eyes blurred as I stumbled over potholes in the drive. He should never have come! If only I'd gone back to London without seeing him, my world would still be intact.

He caught up. 'There will be somebody for you one day, I know, somebody who is a better person than me.'

'Oh, shut up!' It was a relief to feel angry enough to shout at him. 'Can't you see you're only making it worse?'

And that was how we parted. Me, hurrying for home with tears pouring down my face and him, standing at the first bend of the drive - probably staring after me, though I didn't turn around to look. Pitying me, for certain.

Later that morning we went back to London on the train and I began studying for my School Certificate, trying not to think about Swallowcliffe or Andreas Rosenfeld. Schoolwork was a help: I buried my head in my books and studied like never before, from first thing in the morning until late at night. My friends mostly left me alone (probably thinking I'd turned into a real swot) but that was all right - I was too miserable to feel lonely and couldn't be bothered to try and fit in. Sometimes I'd go with my brothers to the Mickey Mouse club at the Odeon on a Saturday morning, or shopping at Woolworth's in the afternoon, but most of the time all I did was prepare for the exams. I couldn't even spare the energy to wonder about Mum and Dr Hathaway, although a letter arrived on the doormat every few days postmarked Edenvale and I guessed he was writing to her.

'Whistle while you work,' the boys sang, 'Mussolini made a shirt, Hitler wore it, Chamberlain tore it, whistle while you work.' War was coming soon, everyone knew that. Mum told me the council was making plans to evacuate city schools into the countryside, teachers along with the children. She was making plans, too, though we didn't discover what they were until the holidays had almost begun. On the evening after my last exam, she sat the three of us down and told us that she'd given in her notice at the school and paid our last month's rent: we'd be moving down to Swallowcliffe at the beginning of the summer holidays.

'You've been nagging me for so long to live in the country that I'm sure you'll be pleased,' she said. Stan and Alfie were already jumping all over the kitchen, waving their arms in the air. 'There are good schools for all of you and we can rent the gate lodge for as long as we want. The boarding school is up and running and I'm going to teach there. Isobel? You are pleased, aren't you?'

I didn't know. At one time, this would have been my dearest wish, but now the thought of having to see Andreas every day was hard to contemplate. And yet, to live at Swallowcliffe, to be a part of the school … what could be more wonderful than that?

And so here we are, the four of us snug in the gate lodge. The boys started school a couple of days ago and so did I: the county school in Hardingbridge. I passed my School Certificate with flying colours so now I'm going on to Highers. 'You might want to teach one day, like me,' Mum says, and perhaps I

Isobel's Story

will. Over the summer holidays, I spent a lot of time helping out at the Hall. The Swallowcliffe School for Refugee Children, that's what it's called now. Not all the children are Jewish: some have parents the Nazis don't like because they're Communists, or people who've spoken out against Hitler. The Hall is full of iron bedsteads and we have more than thirty children sleeping up in the attic, as well as those in the bedrooms; twelve came from Poland last week but most have already been in this country for a while, staying at other hostels. There are English conversation classes, games outside and music all the time. The house is full of laughter and noise, despite the sadness that hangs over everyone and sometimes has to break out. Gran would have loved it and Lord Vye seems delighted. He and the children have settled into the Dower House with Sissy and Mr Huggins, and a new housekeeper we haven't met yet; Lady Vye comes and goes like she always did.

Last week, the Swallowcliffe children gave a concert in the village hall and everybody came; they had to perform three encores and the audience wouldn't stop clapping. Mr Prior's been giving the school twenty pounds of sausages a week since the beginning and the children take it in turns to go out to tea with people like the Murdochs, Mrs Olds and Miss Hartcup. The dire predictions made by the man from London haven't come true so far.

Mr Tarver doesn't live in Stone Martin any

more. One night in the pub, Mrs Olds' son Charlie told a friend that he'd seen the shopkeeper cycling away from the Hall when he was out rabbiting, on the night of the fire. Rumours started spreading and PC Dawes got to hear of them, but before he could ask any questions, Mr Tarver had gone. Eunice said he went to live with his sister in Eastbourne, but Sissy thinks she made that up for want of something to say. As for Eunice: she found a job in the biscuit factory in Hardingbridge, which apparently she likes much better than service or shop work. A new family have arrived to run the village shop and they're friendly enough, although Mum thinks the shelves aren't quite what Mr Tarver's were.

Stan and Alfie spent a lot of time with Tristan over the summer holidays and Dr Hathaway's been teaching them to ride: one of his patients has ponies they can borrow. He and Mum go riding together every weekend and we sometimes have supper together, just like a proper family. That's taken some getting used to but Mum is so happy, it rubs off on the rest of us. She sings around the house these days and she's always smiling.

So you could say that all those impossible things I used to dream about have come true. Except that Gran isn't here any more and Andreas doesn't love me the way I love him. I know he's grateful - his mother arrived in June and maybe I had something to do with that - but gratitude isn't what I want. It's

Isobel's Story

hard for us even to be friends at the moment, I feel so awkward around him.

We'll be friends again one day, though, I'm sure of that. With each day that goes by, I feel stronger in myself. 'You're so young, Izzie,' Mum said the other day, scooping me up in a hug. 'You have your whole life ahead of you. Plenty of wonderful things to come!' And this is such a beautiful, tranquil place to live. On a soft summer evening, Gran's presence seems to be all around me. I'll look down on the house from the Fairview Tower and imagine her there, sitting in her chair by the kitchen window, or hear her voice at unexpected moments inside my head. Whenever I see Mr Chadwick about the Hall, I think of her - and Iris too.

Swallowcliffe has become a place of refuge, and only just in time. After so many months of waiting, it has finally happened. Hitler invaded Poland three days ago and yesterday, England and France declared war on Germany. The younger children haven't realised yet what war means; the rest of us know there'll be no more refugees sailing to safety across the English Channel. All the borders are closed now, and the terrible thing is, Andreas's cousin Gisela is still in Germany. Despite everyone's efforts, she couldn't get out in time. Silence has fallen; there will be no more letters or parcels from home. All we can do is wait, and pray. 'At least we can make these children feel wanted,' Mum says, but what about the others, left behind?

This morning Mum and I watched two little girls chasing each other through the sculpture garden. The sun shone on their hair and they were laughing, which sounded strange on such a sad day. 'That's something to hold on to,' Mum said. 'What if each of those girls grows up to have a family of her own? We must help those who are here now, Izzie, not torture ourselves thinking about what might have been.'

The Hall is our sanctuary. Maybe in time the children we've taken in will learn to be happy here. Perhaps they'll feel the love and laughter that's echoed round these walls for so many years, besides the love their parents are sending from miles away. We did what we could, I suppose. But I can't help asking myself, was it enough?

THE END

About the Author:

Jennie Walters was partly inspired to write the Swallowcliffe Hall series by visits to beautiful old English country houses, including Kingston Lacey in Dorset, Belton House in Lincolnshire and Castle Howard in Yorkshire. As a teenager, she spent two years in a cliff-top boarding school with wood-panelled rooms, a huge marble staircase and one of the largest collections of stuffed birds in England. Much later, finding a silver housekeeper's *châtelaine* when clearing out her father-in-law's flat whetted her interest in Victorian servants and their masters and mistresses, and prompted her to create a fictional country house of her own.

For more information on World War Two and the *Kindertransporte*, including personal stories from survivors, along with a fascinating insight into the world of English country houses and the families and servants who live in them, visit Jennie's website:

www.jenniewalters.com

Printed in Great Britain
by Amazon